Stories From Ou

What women are
Stories From O

"As a mom, designer, partner and friend I rarely have time to read. But for this book, I will make the time. It looks fantastic and it is refreshing to see Canadian women profiled."

Anne Hung
Designer
Anne Hung Boutique

"The concept of this book is amazing. This is a must-have for any woman who has ever dated or been in a relationship. I can't wait to read all of the stories."

Heather Reier
Founder and President
Cake Beauty

"I applaud the strength and courage it takes for young women to tell their stories— I wish I had done it!! Kudos to Carissa and the "Black Book" team for bringing this important collection to life."

Ruth A. Bastedo
President
Continuum Media

"I've always said that every bad date makes for a great story, so I'm excited to see that someone has pulled them together so that we can read, laugh and enjoy them together!"

Joanna Track
Founder & President
Sweetspot.ca

For further information or if you would like to contact
the author/s please write to:
HC SILVER LINING LTD.
#427, 801 KING STREET WEST
TORONTO, ONTARIO
CANADA M5V 3C9
www.silverlining.ws

First printing Nov 2005

10   9   8   7   6   5   4   3   2

STORIES FROM OUR BLACK BOOKS

Edited by

Carissa Reiniger
Sarah Hutchison

silver lining

This book is dedicated to all of the women who have played the dating game. Those who have won and those who are still figuring out how to play.

The Story of
Stories From Our Black Book

"Wow - we have a book?!" Haha. I think we said that about 100 times the night we made the final revisions to the book and sent it off to the printer. Putting this book together has been a wonderful experience for the two of us. It has been a journey full of sleepless nights, hours of pouring over stories, and emails back and forth changing the font on this or the color on that. We have come together with very diverse skill sets and the product is something we are both very proud of.

However, it is the support from women across Canada that has impacted the quality of this project. From media who have jumped on board, to distributors who are planning to carry the book, to all of our contributors (without whom there would be no book), we have been blessed by everyone's excitement and participation.

We didn't know what to expect when we made the open call for stories. Our initial assumption was that it would turn into a disaster date book or a boy bashing anthology. But we were pleasantly surprised. The submissions we have received cover all aspects of relationships: first dates, sex, heartbreak and falling in love. Every woman who wrote a story for this book told us about a very real experience. Genuine emotion has come through in their writing and there is no hiding the joy or pain that the authors bring out in their stories.

The final product is a compilation of 100 stories. You will laugh out loud at some and cry at others. You will feel a connection to every one of them in some way. We did.

We want to thank a couple of people who have been great during this whole process. Thanks to Mike Grand for coming on board and believing in this project enough to invest in it. Thanks to Adam Duguay and Tenth Floor Visual Graphics for putting up with our demanding and picky changes to the cover - your patience and fabulous work is greatly appreciated! Thanks to Erika Baltrus who stepped in as our second set of eyes and who did a final proofread of all 100 stories before going to the printer. And, thanks to Jennifer Parks of Sun Media. She saw a story in *Stories From Our Black Books* before we had gathered our first story. Her coverage was instrumental in the quick success of the book.

We would also like to thank the women who have helped us turn a concept into a reality. Dinah Dief – Project Manager, Karen Henderson – Logistics Coordinator, and Aja Whitfield – Project Coordinator.

Also, thank you to the partners who have come on board for this book. It is with great pleasure that we can offer our readers gifts from them and information about their products and services in the back of our book. Special thanks to INDU for giving Carissa the most perfect gift: a new wardrobe for the book launch and fabulous image consulting. Thanks to Heather at Cake for being a great friend and professional ally. Thanks to Amber, Karen, Allison, and Faye; clients of Silver Lining who have become friends. We are so happy to be working with you and wish you the best of luck with Relax and ALI. We will make them both wonderfully successful! To the girls at Rethink Breast Cancer, we hope that the awareness and money raised through the release of this book will impact the pivotal work you do. To the ladies at Women Entrepreneurs of Canada, there is honor in being part of this group. We hope that this book will encourage many more talented entrepreneurs across Canada. To Sara at Sister, Joanna at Sweetspot.ca, Rima at Serve

This! and Carolina at Sheshoppe.ca, it is great to have you as partners on this. We look forward to continuing alliances and successes with each of you.

So, Ladies. Read and enjoy. Make sure you take advantage of the many offers from our partners and enjoy the real life stories from our contributors. Remember, these women are just like you. *Stories From Our Black Books* gives you a glimpse into 100 women's lives, each at different stages and with individual experiences, but each on the same journey.

Enjoy your journey!

Carissa and Sarah

STORIES FROM OUR
BLACK BOOKS

Prologue

Our first story offers some advice to our readers…

My advice to offer dating women:

I am the only woman in a power plant. I have worked with fifteen men for over ten years now. They range in age from 35 to their mid 50's, but some were in their 20's when we first started to work together. I tell all my girlfriends that I know MORE than the average woman wants to know about how the male mind works, and trust me girls - it's really VERY simple!

If you want to catch a guy's interest and move beyond that first date you need to know this. Men are basic creatures and have three needs. The first two relate to Maslow's theory - food and sex! The third is their area of 'interest'. You need to find out the one thing that turns a guy on. For some it's cars, for others it's a sport (or sports in general), for others it could be wines, computers, or games. You catch my drift.

It really makes it very simple for you then. What you do is become knowledgeable in that area. You don't want to become an expert - God knows - he wouldn't want to hang out with you if you knew more or were better than him at HIS thing. But if it's something he can share, discuss intelligently with you, or do with you, then you've got him hooked!

I met my hubby playing golf - a sport he loves (and fortunately - so do I). I'm not a great golfer but I know the rules and can keep up with the average male. Sometimes my husband shoots a better score than I do - sometimes I do better than he does (I can't let him think he's THAT good!). But it's something we can do together, laugh, and talk about during and after. After all, you have to have SOMETHING to do and talk about after the other two things are taken care of!

Lori, 47

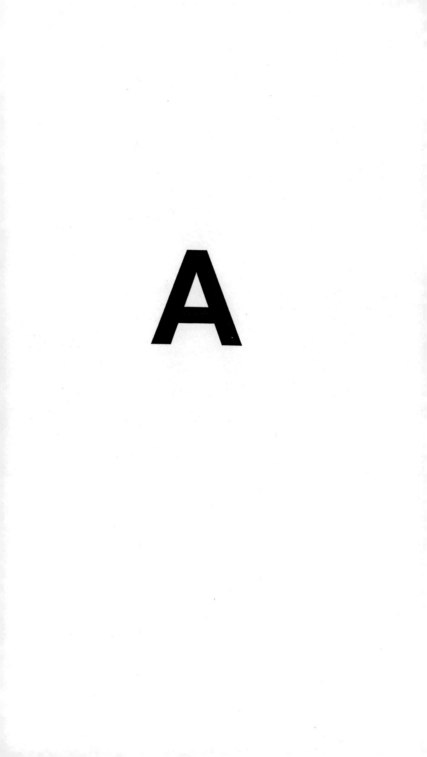

Alan....

A while ago I was "seeing" a guy called Alan. He seemed like a nice guy and I was quite smitten with him. Anyway after "seeing" each other for about a month I had to go on a school trip for a week. Alan hadn't text messaged me for a few days so I was focused on having a good time with my friends. About four days into the trip I got this text message that said, and I quote; "Hey how's your trip? Just wanted to let you know that my ex-girlfriend is pregnant. Have a nice day."

HAVE A NICE DAY!!!! No joke, that's what he wrote. He tells me his ex is pregnant via a text message and then he says HAVE A NICE DAY!!!!

Anonymous

Adam....

"Now I know what I don't want...I learned that with you" - Leslie Feist

The worst year of my life was my 28th year. This is the year that Saturn Returns. It is a period in everyone's life that, theoretically, one is supposed to experience a time of change and upheaval. Well, in my 28th year, Saturn returned with a vengeance on my ass.

I was in the second year of a relationship that should have ended at my 28th birthday. Amid the various counts of distasteful, disrespectful behaviour on Adam's part he was, and is, an addict and a manipulator.

Silver Lining

The first indication of things to come occurred the day Adam and I were moving in together, in the fall of 2003. The night before he was nowhere to be found, and in the morning he still wasn't answering my phone calls. When he finally decided to get in contact with me, around noon or so, I was venting over eggs with a girlfriend and seriously considering finding a place on my own. How could I live with someone so irresponsible?

We met a few hours later to discuss things. I threatened it was over if he did not stop his excessive abuse of booze and drugs. He begged and cried. He told me that I was extremely important to him and that he would stop.

He didn't stop, and after a while it was like I was on drugs myself. The highs were so amazing and the lows were incredibly painful. It was truly a vicious cycle. It was the highs that kept me in it I guess, like making dinners together, and spending time with his lovely parents.

I lost my trust in everything that year. I was moody from lack of sleep and crying my eyes out. I also had little patience for the challenges that came along with starting my own business.

I asked Adam to move out in the spring of 2004 but we kept seeing each other all summer with his Jekyll- and-Hyde routine in full effect.

By the end of 2004 I was exhausted and I knew I did not want to be involved with Adam anymore. I think he sensed how I was feeling. I was out of the country for the holidays, and being the sadistic jerk that he was, he decided to profess that he "missed me" and that he "was in love" with me. He was effectively reeling me back in.

18

When I returned to Canada I told him not to bother me if he was going to continue to blow his brains out every week. Naturally he said it would not be an issue and I bought it. Hook, line, and sinker!

Of course, the relationship came to a bitter end less than a week later. He basically asked me to put my life on hold while he "figured things out." When I realized that he was still committed to the party scene, and that I did not fit in, I finally walked away (with some self-respect intact). How stupid was I to trust Adam? I asked my friends and family to get behind me once again because he wanted to "work it out." It was all so tough to swallow.

Thankfully I've now worked through it with the support of amazing friendships and now I have a blossoming business to concentrate on.

Lessons Learned…

It took me a long time to come to terms with the way Adam was, is, and always will be. People don't change unless they want to and you can't make them change. It did not matter how much love, caring, or sacrificing I did on my part; I was never going to receive that same devotion, support, and sacrifice in return.

I learned a lot in my 28th year of life. What I went through I would not wish on anyone. I thought I was losing my mind and I suffered from horrible heartache. That is what a manipulator will do to you.

I don't see him around anymore, but people will mention his name. Some wonder why I was with someone like him. Love can be so blind. I now know that love should not be so difficult. I know now that I don't want to have to wonder when I wake up at 5 a.m., on a Wednesday, and he's not there beside me, where my supposed best friend and life partner is.

I ignored my gut feelings for too long and suffered. Why? I knew the signs. I have a history of abuse in my own family. But I know why. I wanted to save Adam from himself. I see now that this was not my responsibility. I tried, and Lord knows I made my mistakes in the relationship, but as life moves along you realize what a waste of time it is to try so hard to make the good in someone eclipse the bad.

When I talk to my friends about their various relationship troubles I am not negative. I only urge them to listen to what his or her gut is saying about the person. And if that person is only going to hurt you, or make you cry, or lay blame and make you feel bad about yourself, then I say CUT THEM OUT OF YOUR LIFE.

As humans, we can only move on, learn from our mistakes, and realize that we deserve better. And better is out there...I am sure of it!

Vanessa, 29

Alain....

Our longest date was nine-hundred-and-eighty-four hours and eight provinces long. Together we drove from one end of the country to the other, and we went through everything in between. He put up with my varying moods. He enthusiastically met every member of my VERY extended family. He was even willing to listen to my favourite Shania Twain song far too many times. After all that, Alain is still smiling, which is a miracle.

True love is driving with somebody for ten hours straight and still finding something to laugh about at the end of the day. True love is putting up with many unplanned bathroom stops. True love is getting completely lost, but knowing that together you'll find your way back to the right path.

Evelyn, 23

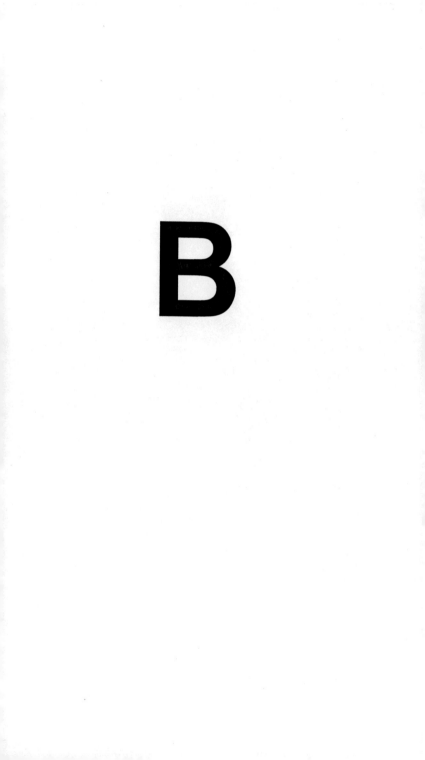

B

Bobby....

Remember in the movie, *Thelma and Louise*, when Thelma (Geena Davis) says, "Now I understand what all the fuss is about!" after she has sex with J.D. (Brad Pitt)? We all need a J.D. Bobby was my J.D.

Johanna, 24

Buddy....

Meticulously folded in behind four neatly placed rows of cotton bikini briefs, is where I keep my underwear. My favourite pair comes from France, a silk bra and panty set reserved for special dates ONLY. Further down the drawer I keep my matching pink lycra and cotton blend set, these I like to wear when I practice Yoga. G-strings come next, and I wear those with my low-rider jeans, the jeans that say to the world, don't mess with me today! And then of course the Grannies in the very back of the drawer...you know, the ones set aside for "Aunt RED's" monthly visit. Ahhhh...the underwear drawer.

In my spare time, when I'm NOT organizing my underwear drawer, you can usually find me surfing on-line. I love the convenience of Internet dating! I can choose who I want to date and where and when I want to meet them. The only downside to using the Internet as a dating tool is that just like the Charmin, "You can't squeeze before you buy."

He went by the user-name, 'Buddy'. We arranged to meet in his neighbourhood. I arrived well equipped for any emergency-type situation that might arise. I had a charged cell-phone and my debit card. Then the moment of truth presented itself. He stepped out of his souped-up, late 80's sports car, and immediately it became clear to me that he had lied about his height AND his girth. He did however have a cute smile and funky Elvis-style side-burns…cute enough to attract my attention.

Have an open mind, I reminded myself as we chatted over a glass of merlot in the first bar of his choice. Forty-five minutes later, on our way to the second bar of his choice he nonchalantly pulled out a joint.

"You wanna smoke?" he said.

"No thanks," I replied.

Excuse me! Who offers a girl pot on a first date?

We ended up at the bar, a drinking room and pool hall off the beaten path in Toronto's Parkdale area. We played a few games and then chatted on the snakeskin covered couches. While I had switched to drinking ginger ale, Buddy switched to vodka. He mentioned to me that he was back in school finishing up his second degree. By the look of his starving artist, Salvation Army type fashion statement, I at least found comfort in the fact that he hadn't lied about his current income. He didn't have one!

A little while later I felt like dancing. He suggested a bar with a live band across the street. When we got there he informed me that he had no more money left.

Of course you have no money left. You spent it all on vodka!

I offered to pay the cover and in we went. Of course the band was horrible and every other word out of the lead singer's mouth was f _ _ _. And no, it wasn't the word fork. "Fork" would have been funny. "Fork" would have been danceable! So I wasn't drinking, I wasn't dancing; I wasn't even smiling any more! It was time for me to end this pathetic date and head home.

At 12:35 a.m. the woman in me took over and told this lame-o, Grunge-Beastie-wanna-be boy, that I had an early appointment the next morning and it was time for me to head home. Oh, but stick around readers. The most outrageous part of the date is still to come!

So now we're walking back through the slushy, cold-layered streets of Parkdale. Back to his territory and, more importantly, back to my car and my ticket out. But on the way he actually had the audacity to try and slip me the ecstasy pill! I watched as he slithered his hand inside the pocket of his worn leather jacket, from which he pulled out a thin, silver case the size of a cigarette package - the kind you'd imagine a gangster to have. Then he slid the sleek, metal side-hatch open, and onto the palm of his sweaty hand he dropped a small, white pill. It was not a Tylenol, believe me! I've been around the rave scene and party crowds. I knew immediately that it was ecstasy. And although I am no dating expert, I feel confident in saying that being offered drugs on a first date is pretty much a deal-breaker. Needless to say, Buddy didn't qualify for a second date. If he ever calls again I'll probably just tell him I have plans to organize my underwear drawer.

Shoe, 34

Blake....

I was quite excited when I started dating Blake. I'd had a crush on him for years. After he officially became my boyfriend, I invited him to have dinner with my family. It just so happened that it was my birthday dinner and my grandparents were in town. I was nervous about my family's reaction to Blake's blue hair, but he won them all over with ease. Everything was going really well until I noticed that Blake had hardly taken a bite of his lasagna but instead had eaten half his napkin. I kept quiet hoping that it would go unnoticed. No such luck. In the middle of the conversation my sister stopped and looked at him with an expression of confusion and humour on her face. "Are you eating your napkin?" Damn.

Erin, 22

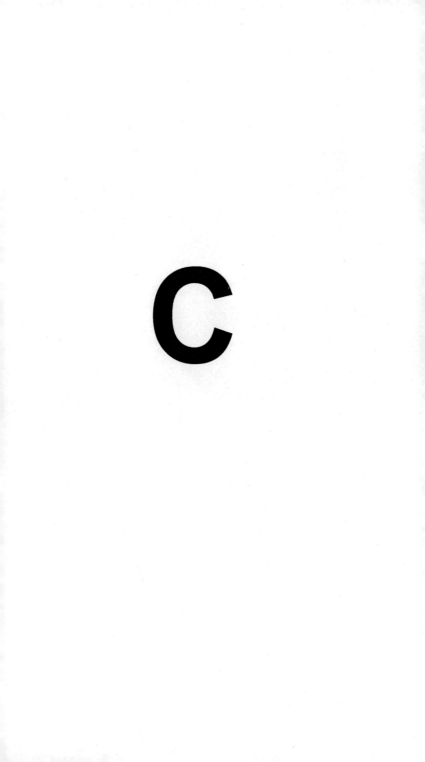

Clive....

Mom, bless her enthusiastic heart, carries a picture of me on her keychain and canvasses on my behalf. She's a competitive golfer who's trying to find the perfect match for me and hit the longest drive. A great day for her would be getting on the green and finding me Mr. Right.

She thought that in Clive she had succeeded. She showed him my picture; he showed her his portfolio (he models when he's not busy being a golf pro). I gave approval (who the heck wouldn't?) and he phoned.

He was pretty, all long, lean, sculpted, groomed, sleek and blow-dried. But a very odd boy he turned out to be...

I had a girlfriend once, he confided, his long lashes fluttering, and we did very naughty things.

Oh yes? Such as?

Turned out he had kissed her a couple of times.

Don't ever touch my hair, he said.

I won't, I assured him. It looks lovely, I added a bit weakly, feeling the need to say something.

Sometimes I put it in pigtails and call myself Cathy, he said.

When I got home I told Mom to slow down for while.

Lisa, 27

Chris....

We had been married not even a year, but I was becoming self-conscious that my body was starting to change shape and get larger since our honeymoon. I knew Chris must have noticed, it's hard to hide things like that at all times. I wasn't sure when to bring the subject up. It was becoming a struggle for me and my thoughts were filled with what he might be thinking. Finally, I got up the nerve to bring it up after a day of healthy eating and a good run. "I've been gaining weight and I am really unhappy about it..."

His response was perfect for my insecure heart. "You know, we're not going to look like this forever anyway. Think of how we'll look when we're old and everything will be saggy and hairy. We're going to think we looked great at this time in our lives!" He made me laugh, and then he said, "You will *always* be sexy to me!" The way he looked at me when he said it, I really believed him.

Knowing he thought I was sexy made me feel so much better about myself. I started to take even more care of myself because there wasn't so much pressure and guilt to lose weight and look good. My husband would love me however I looked. I wanted to look good for him, and feel good for me.

Janet, 26

Colin....

I had hit my thirties and was craving sex – lots of sex.

I hadn't seen any action for more than a year-and-a-half and I had been quite content without it. So I was surprised when one spring day my body suddenly ached for it.

Up until that point I had only had three partners, all of whom I had been in long-term relationships with. Unfortunately, none of my experiences with those men would qualify as mind-blowing sex. I realized I was still harbouring some hang-ups from my youth and decided to tackle some of my sexual issues. My plan had two components. The first was to take some workshops at a local sex store to give me confidence and make me feel more comfortable with myself. The second component was to find myself an 'FB' or 'F*ck Buddy'.

As luck would have it, a potential 'FB' moved into my building. Colin was ten years younger than me and incredibly flirtatious. At first I was constantly dropping hints about my age and the fact that I was older than I looked, but that didn't seem to deter him. In some ways it was the perfect situation. Because of the age difference I would never consider him a potential mate. Therefore, I could enjoy guilt-free, no-strings-attached sex. Plus, Colin only lived one floor above me so you couldn't beat the situation in terms of convenience. After an outrageous flirtation for about six weeks we started a wild sexual relationship. We developed a system where we would leave coloured sticky notes on the banister of the stairs to indicate if this was a good time or not. My friends still laugh when I talk about my young 'sticky' boy.

The sex was excellent and definitely better than anything I had ever experienced before. It gave me a chance to practice some techniques I had learned at my sex workshops. But what I wasn't prepared for was the emptiness that came afterwards. Somehow the intimacy of the act made it evident that there was absolutely no emotional connection between us. I realized that I wasn't cut out for a purely physical relationship. More importantly, I knew I deserved more.

My affair with Colin lasted about a month and then fizzled out about as quickly as it began. I don't have any regrets. It was exactly the fling I needed. Luckily we don't run into each other very often at the apartment, which was the one component of the fling I didn't really think through. Despite the convenience it's probably not a smart idea to find a 'FB' who lives in the same building as you.

Kathryn, 32

C....

It was my first year of university. I saw him during frosh week. He was handsome. He was wearing a frosh t-shirt. He was partying like a mad man. Our school pub was named 'The Blind Duck', and someone had scrawled 'Big Daddy Duck' across his t-shirt. I had to laugh. I had to comment. I had to flirt. By the end of the night, I had to admit that I had developed a huge crush on him.

A few weeks later a group of us went to a Karaoke bar. I sat beside him. I drank a bit. He drank a bit. We held hands under the table. Like secret lovers we hid our hands from our friends, caressing each other's fingers, burning with excitement. I laughed at something he said. I leaned over. "Kiss me," I demanded. And he did.

He was caring, he was gentle, he was sensitive, passionate, and political. He was nothing like the boys I had dated in the small rural town where I grew up. I fell for him. I fell for him fast. I fell for him hard.

"I love you," "No, I love you," we would whisper in the darkness of the bedroom. And then we would giggle, nuzzling each other's necks and faces, stretching our bodies, skin against skin.

We went camping in Quebec and watched deer one meter away from us, eating the leaves off a tree. We held each other in the quiet, encompassed by the beauty, the magnificence of nature, and knew that we had found our soul mate in one another.

School became a catalyst for our relationship. We were studying completely different subjects but we told each other about what we were learning. We debated each other – young, naive, and stubborn. We were angry at the world, and at the same time we were bedazzled by it, by its people, by our own love.

The first summer we spent apart he bought me a cell phone so we could keep in touch. I was a camp counselor, and I would sit on the stairs of my cabin, utterly exhausted, and seven hours away from one another we would whisper, "I love you," and "No, I love you." A world away, and he remained my lifeline.

Three years of friendship and love. Three years of adventures, tears, laughter. Three years of family dinners, of tying friendships together. Three years, and then we broke up.

It was a slow transition, but we started fighting. A lot. Fights that would last upwards of two hours, fights that left us physically exhausted and emotionally battered. The situation was ugly; we were ugly, no longer bringing out the best in one another. He thought I was too angry. He thought I was depressed. He was right. I thought he was angry. I thought he smoked too much dope. I was right.

We broke up in the fall of our fourth year of university. We fought and he stormed down my stairs. "It's over," I screamed down at him, standing on the landing. I'd threatened so many times before this, but something in my tone made him stop. He turned around, suddenly calm. Sad. "Are you serious?" "Yes," I replied. Crying. Both of us, tears streaming down our faces.

When he walked out the door I knocked on my roommate's door, and when she opened it, I crumpled at her feet. Sobs wracked my body. I had never been so devastated. I had never been so calm and sure of a decision in my life. Though I still loved C., and I knew that I always would, I no longer had to deal with the anger, the poison, and the toxicity that we had created and sustained in our relationship. I just had to deal with the aftermath of it all.

Looking back, through the wonderful looking glass that time creates it is easy to see that there were a multitude of reasons why C. and I broke up. I was afraid of the amount of drugs that he smoked. Not of the drug itself, necessarily, but of the increasing dependence he seemed to have on it over the years. I had asked him to quit, a number of times, and he hadn't, or couldn't as it turned out. There is a certain lack of respect for oneself that accompanies an addiction, and I increasingly lost my admiration for him as I watched him sink deeper into denial.

On my end, I started to battle depression in my second year of university, although I wouldn't identify it as such until three years later. My anger raged out of control. My mood swings were intolerable. I cried for seemingly no reason. I took it out on C. and between the two of us we tumbled into a vicious cycle of dependency and rejection.

Throughout our long and drawn-out break-up I mourned the loss of my best friend. More than anything I missed C's companionship. I sought counseling immediately after our break-up. I remember calling him up, six months later, to talk to him about some things I was sorting out in my counseling sessions. I was crying, I was shaken up, and despite our separation, he listened to me and gave me advice. We had shared so much during our three years together that he was the only one that truly understood what I was going through. I didn't have to explain my past to him, the details of my family. He already knew. He still cared.

Somewhere, deep in my heart, I thought we might get back together. "Someday, when we're both better," I would say to myself. "Someday, when we're both happier, with ourselves, with life. When we're more stable," I would say to him in moments of complete honesty, over the phone or in emails.

Our contact was sporadic and punctuated by long periods of silence. At one point, after he started to date one of my 'good' friends, I wrote him and told him to "never contact me again." We both dated other people, but we had the same circle of friends and I would see him at social events. It was awkward and I was always shaken to my toes every time I had an exchange with him. I knew in my guts that I still loved him. But I felt that I was on a road to happiness, and he was stuck in the same dank existence.

Then there was a death in my family and I received an email in my in-box. He wrote little, but he didn't have to say much. He cared, he always had. More than anyone in my life, he understood the complexity of my family, and reached out with the right words to offer.

Four months later we had both broken up with the people we had been dating. Our mutual friends planned a trip to Ottawa for the long weekend. We both went and there was electricity in the air. We felt it, we acknowledged it, and with a fear for the unknown in the pit of my stomach, I jumped into a situation so familiar, yet so unknown.

Silver Lining

Our first date after the long weekend he made dinner for me at his house. Music, candles, and wine – I was excited to say the least. He had always been romantic, and our two years apart had only refined his gestures.

There we sat, in his apartment, terrified of each other. We had so many questions to ask each other, and so many reservations. We had caused each other so much pain, and yet this love, this dangerously passionate love, stilled raged inside us...

It is hard to describe our relationship now. We have both grown up. We have conquered our demons. Yet our lives continually change us and move us in different directions. The time we spent apart has taught us to be independent. Neither one of us is now afraid to be alone. There is tranquility, maturity, to our love. And yet, our love is fierce, and raw. I would walk through fire for him and I know he would do the same for me. We have the same goals, the same dreams, and the same moral values. He remains, to this day, my best friend. Words cannot describe how lucky I feel to have him in my life.

A love lost, a love regained. Trust time...

S.J., 24

Cam....

He was right and I was wrong...that's how it all got started. At least that's how he remembers it.

Cam and I met on a job site about six years ago and he started asking me out right away. I declined many times with all of the excuses that we commonly use, "I don't even know him," or "I don't date people I work with," or "He's not my type."

I left the job after a few months but still kept in contact with Cam with some help from mutual friends who had started dating. Cam was very persistent, but I was convinced that it wouldn't work out. I thought he was great - as a friend. After a while Cam kind of gave up on me (do you blame him!?) and I didn't see him as much after that.

All of a sudden, when he wasn't in my life, I realized that I missed him. I loved spending time with him, he made me laugh, and we got along so well. But by then I was sure it was too late and I had messed it up. I decided to swallow my pride and call Cam, hoping that this time he wouldn't be the one making excuses. I found out he was still interested and he would give me, and us, another chance.

We have been together ever since then and are now very much in love. We have been married for two years. So, for all those girls out there looking for their 'type' and steering clear of all the others...you may be all wrong about your true 'Mr. Right.'

Brenda, 30

Charles....

The Professional Window Man

I saw Charles today at lunch. I was leaning across a counter in the Food Court and he was in line behind me. I feel terribly vulnerable when people stand behind me as they have a full view of the broad horizon that I like to pretend isn't there.

I turned around and saw him and for an instant I thought that at the sight of me he would rush, gather me into his beautiful arms, and propose marriage.

Instead he stiffened his jaw and concentrated intently on his life and the sandwich at hand, both of which were of equal magnitude to him I am sure. I am a hopeless romantic and still believe there is a future for us. I can't honestly believe he doesn't like me even after everything I said to him. He should have appreciated my acerbic wit and not taken it so personally. That's the trouble with accountants; they have no sense of humour. The new breed cut their hair fashionably, wear antique watches and cufflinks but their blandness is stronger than their aftershave. Where I always go wrong is that I firmly believe that when I confront a person with his inadequacies that the said inadequacies will be replaced by the perfection I am seeking.

Oh, they will say, so that's what you wanted. I am so glad you pointed it out. Let me be that person immediately!

So, when I told Charles that he didn't have a personality, I wasn't being insulting or impolite, I was just hoping he would develop the personality I knew was there. Somewhere.

Instead he was deeply insulted.

After our first date I didn't hear from him for six weeks. He would come to the window of his office building across from me and he would gaze at me while I would laugh and pretend to be famous, happy, and well loved. After a month of his gazing but not calling, I decided to give up. And then, what do you know, he appeared at my front doorstep and invited me to lunch. I was busy, thank heavens, and on my way out. How uncool to be available with no notice.

He was wearing jeans and a white shirt, nothing unusual. But pinned to his gorgeous chest was a small tin sheriff's badge, the kind that little boys wear. Not your standard designer attire. I was a bit disconcerted especially when he started shooting imaginary rounds at my dog and I thought his behaviour was a bit odd, but I was too overcome by flattery to be concerned. I mean the man had actually come to visit me, and all by himself.

After that nothing happened for three weeks. Then he invited me to his home for dinner. He read to me from *The Place of the Dead Roads* by W. Burroughs. He played Mister Heartbreak and it all made sense. Charles saw himself as a modern-day cowboy, desired by all, the professional Mr. Heartbreaker. I leaned back in my chair and stared up into the night sky. Who was I to stand in the way of a man's fantasies? I found it admirable that he had such a well-thought out game plan.

So what went wrong? He said, while playing with the cuff of his shirtsleeve, that he knew that I wanted to have sex with him and that's why I had been such a bitch.

I said, yes, well that's because you have no personality. I said he should either develop personality or leave my life. What I meant was "Please assume the personality that I want you to have." He chose to leave my life instead.

I phoned his home on various occasions and eventually he installed an answering machine. I am miserable now. Mostly because he could so easily have been what I wanted, his face was perfect. If he asked me today, I would marry him tomorrow. At least I know that he would leave me alone. He is great to watch movies with and waitresses love him. These are, I believe, good reasons as any for marriage. And if I were married I would never have to worry about what to do on weekends again. Wow, imagine that

Silver Lining

freedom…

Being single, I plan lunches, dinners, drinks, and movies – anything and everything in a desperate attempt to ward off the boredom factor. I can only relax if I have planned weeks ahead.

I let my mind play with one of its favourite fantasies:

I am staring at the hubcap of an expensive car. A man approaches. Of course he is perfect in every way.

Do you like it? he asks.

I answer yes.

You can have it if you marry me, he says. And we live happily ever after.

Or there is the guy who takes me to lunch and hands me a string of credit cards. I tell him that if he gives them to me I will not hesitate to use them. It turns out that if I spend more than any of my predecessors (which I do) then he will know it's true love and we will live happily ever after.

I know my fantasies are boring and superficial but I am starved of men and money. It's been so long since I have had either.

Time to plan the evening's pub-crawl. I must remember to avoid accountants at all costs.

Lisa, 27

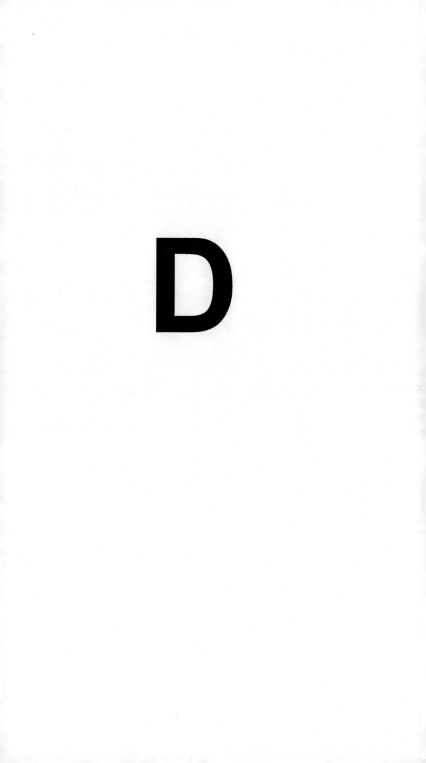

D

Drew....

Once upon a time, I went on a few dates with a guy named Drew. He was nice enough; charming, sweet, and really into me. A perfect recipe for summer love! As we made plans for a beautiful Sunday night in June, he suggested that I should have a BBQ. I hadn't offered, so I found it a little forward that he was suggesting that I BBQ for him. But I was into this guy and so I thought, "Why not?"

I should tell you that Drew is a picky eater. If there was one thing I learned about him on our first three dates, it was that he was allergic to butter and he hated veggies. In preparation for the BBQ, I went to the St. Lawrence Market on Saturday to pick up some souvlakis. As I was walking around, I started stressing over a side dish. Drew is a meat and potato person, and I don't eat potatoes. But being the gem that I am, I decided to make him scalloped potatoes and potato salad to go with the meat.

Drew arrived at 4:00 p.m. on Sunday to hang out and have dinner. I decided to start making the scalloped potatoes. They would take a while and we had lots of time before I needed to fire up the BBQ for the souvlakis. As I reached into the fridge and pulled out the milk, Drew said, "What are you doing?"

Confused, I asked him what he meant, and he said, "What are you doing with the milk?"

"Making scalloped potatoes, and you need milk to make them. You're only allergic to butter and margarine, right?"

"Yeah, but I don't like anything creamy, and well, saucy -- so don't bother making scalloped potatoes. What else do you have?"

"I have potato salad for you. I don't eat potatoes, so I will be having Greek salad -- which you don't like -- instead."

I thought he was acting a little too familiar. We had only been out three times by this point. It was not as though we had been to each other's house, or even gone beyond kissing, so I was surprised that he was so forward, but I let his rudeness pass. When I started preparing to BBQ, he looked at the souvlakis and said, "Where are the hamburgers and hotdogs? I thought this was a BBQ!"

Annoyed by his candor, I told him that McDonalds and Harveys were right around the corner if he wanted hamburgers. By this point, I had had enough, but I consoled myself with the thought that at least he had brought a bottle of wine and some ice cream!

When the souvlakis were ready, Drew insisted that we eat in front of the television. Now generally eating in front of the television is fine, but as I mentioned earlier we didn't really know each other all that well. He grabbed my remote and started watching entertainment news! Dude, I can do this by myself, why are you here?

After we finished eating, I suggested that we see an early movie. I am thinking BIG PICTURE here. Perfect. I will be home by 9:00 p.m. I will be in bed nice and early, and I will forget that this date ever happened! As I am looking for movie listing times, he says, "Wow, your hair!" I thought maybe this guy would redeem himself and pay me a nice compliment, but he continues, "I cannot get over how dark your roots are!"

We saw, *Fast and Furious 2*, an action-packed movie full of cars, babes, and lots of testosterone. I made him pay for the movie. I had already paid for dinner! During the movie, I looked over and saw my date sleeping. As he started to snore, I checked my watch. It was 7:00 p.m. I figured I would let him sleep. That way he wasn't bothering me, and I could pretend that I came to see the movie by myself.

It was still daylight when the movie was finally over. So, as he dropped me off at home, I used the *Two-Prong Approach*. I had a big attack of fake coughing to avoid the kiss, and then gave him a hug goodbye instead. I literally said, "Good-bye, Drew. It was nice knowing you." As I got out of the car and walked into my place, I reflected that the single life had its good and bad points, and that leaving Drew behind was definitely one of the good points.

Kathy, 30

Dino....

You know you are in dating trouble when your boyfriend's car is cleaner than your bedroom and he uses more hair-care products than you do.

You're also in dating trouble when your date invites you to dinner - at his parent home, where he lives. He serves pizza out of a box. When you ask him what he is thinking about, he says he is thinking about where he can have sex with you after dinner. You know you are really in trouble when you think, "Good question."

Heather, 46

David....

I moved to Kingston with my Dad and Mom five-and-a-half years ago. We started attending a church in the city and that is where I met David.

David had a friend named Jay. The three of us hit it off right away and became instant friends. I also had a little thing for Jay, and David always tried to get me to tell him, but I never did. We all hung out all the time. Jay then got word that he had been accepted into the army full-time and would be posted a few hours away. I was a little sad but I moved on. Then there were two.

David and I now became a little closer. We would go to social events together, we would watch movies together, and when we would watch movies together we would sit really close to one another and maybe, just maybe, we'd hang onto hands. There was great suspicion about the two of us, but we denied all rumours.

One Sunday night after church we all went out to a friend's house. One of David's friends was down from Toronto and needed a ride back home, so David offered to drive him and asked me to come along. On the way back to Kingston we were hanging onto hands. If any of you know me you know that I don't hold back and what I say is never sugar coated, so I came right out and asked, "What's going on with us? Is this ever going to turn into something more? Are you wasting my time?" Poor guy, he probably felt bombarded with questions that he wasn't prepared to answer. I suggested that we pull off the highway so we could talk more about this. We did, and at a car park somewhere between Toronto and Kingston the two of us decided our future.

He said he had a problem with the age difference (there is seven years between us). I laughed and said, "Is that what's holding you back?" We decided that we would 'test drive' the relationship and while we were doing that we wouldn't tell anyone else about us. We didn't tell anyone about us for about four months. I finally got fed up and asked when we were going to start telling people. I said if we didn't decide soon, I was going to say, "Bye-Bye." So he agreed and we let everyone know.

On our three-and-a-half year anniversary he asked me to marry him. Of course I said yes and we got married five months later on January 24, 2004. We have now been married for a year-and-a-half. I absolutely love being married to him. He is an amazing man. I can't wait for what the future has in store for us.

Ladies and Gentleman, if you marry your best friend, you cannot go wrong. David and I constantly laugh and have a great time with one another. I hope that this story may inspire some of you who haven't found your true love. They are out there, you just have to keep looking.

Brianne, 23

Devon....

I was married when I was 19-years-old to Robin. I had known Robin since I was twelve. We had a daughter together, but before she turned three, we were divorced. We remained divorced for ten years but we were on again / off again. When I was 30-years-old, I found the Lord. At that time, Robin and I were living together and we had added a son to our family. I wasn't sure where I stood with the Lord, so I decided to ask God about my situation. He made it very clear that

Silver Lining

I should move out.

I was glad I listened because several days later I found out that Robin had been having an affair at work. The children and I were on welfare, but I had a Christian couple as landlords in the complex where we lived. They were incredible to me. They helped me with food when I was short and sold me a vehicle for $1.00 when I needed one. Less than three years later, Robin went forward at a crusade and gave his life to Christ. We were re-married on Thanksgiving Day in 1979. One of our friends who had first shared the gospel with us gave us our wedding reception. I was thrilled and couldn't have been happier.

However, something was not right. I kept it to myself because God had truly used our situation to share with others and encourage them if their marriage was on shaky ground. Robin was reading the Bible upwards of twelve to sixteen hours a day, but he would not take any advice from anyone. He felt he had so much Light that he couldn't tolerate the Darkness around him. He was increasingly critical of pastors and other Christian leaders and he could not settle on a church. I grew increasingly unhappy and fearful. Robin felt that he was responsible to God for my spiritual walk and took the term "submit" very seriously. He became cruel in the way he dealt with our two children.

Then my girlfriend Linda and her two children were in trouble and needed a temporary place to stay while they sold their house. Two-and-a-half years later, they were still with us. Robin and her spent so much time together while I was at work that people thought she was his wife. My depression got so bad that I became suicidal. A friend came to rescue me and encourage me to come back to church, which I did. I then confronted Robin and asked him to make his choice, which he did. He and Linda are now married.

Some ten years after our divorce, I met Devon at a church singles group. We were married almost fourteen years ago. He is very kind and gentle and has been a wonderful husband. The best part is that he's seventeen years younger than me!

Denise, 59

D....

My first date with D. was in MacDonald's. We ordered coffee and proceeded to engage in four hours of intense conversation. Both our marriages had recently broken up, and we were through the initial grieving process and looking to meet someone new. We had met years before through a mutual friend, and so we were not strangers to one another. D. walked me home that night and asked if he could take me out to dinner and the theatre the following week. I readily agreed.

When he came to pick me up, he brought me flowers – fire engine red gladiolas, a huge bunch – and I almost burst into tears. It was years since anyone had brought me flowers! But the best was yet to come. He escorted me to his car and opened the passenger door for me. I was stunned. My ex-husband had never opened doors for me, and would have considered it politically incorrect to do so. As I stepped into D.'s car, I felt like a 'lady' for the first time in a long time. The evening continued to be sublime.

The kindness and consideration that D. showed me on our first date continued as he came to know me better. He never took me for granted. In time we married, and I can honestly say that we are more in love now than ever before. We celebrated our 19th wedding anniversary this year and hope for many more. D.

made a wonderful first impression on me. He treated me as though I was special, as though I was the most cherished woman in the world. And throughout our marriage, for better and for worse, he has never failed to tell me every single day that he loves me and that I am a wonderful wife (even when I'm not). D. has kept the romance alive in our marriage through children, financial crisis, and the ups and downs of everyday living. He is a true romantic, and it goes without saying that I love him dearly in return.

Anonymous, 52

Dan....

I met Dan at a rock show, where a mutual friend introduced us. We hit it off straight away and we were dating within a couple of weeks. I let him dictate most of the rules of our relationship. He was the first to say those three little words, and eventually he was the one to end it.

Despite all the pain and confusion of the aftermath, I picked up his calls and let him see me. After a few months I tried dating someone else, but it didn't work out. Soon after that, Dan started seeing other people, lots of them. It broke my heart again so I decided to make a clean break and moved away.

After a year Dan got back in touch. At first I didn't respond, but he was so friendly I gave him a second chance. It wasn't until six months later that he bothered to tell me he'd had a girlfriend the whole time. He knew I was vulnerable but took advantage of my good nature anyway.

The lesson I have learnt and keenly pass along to my girlfriends is that even seemingly nice men can take advantage of our hearts. But on the positive side, if we have to compromise and let them dictate everything, then maybe they're not the right man for us after all.

Alice, 23

Dave....

My husband and I met when I was 12
He was the canoeing instructor
I was the star student
True love—
That was 1987
I wrote him everyday for a year
Then I turned 13 and gave up.
 I thought about him about nine years later
And called him
He had the same phone number—picked up—and he remembered me—
Then he called me and asked if I could send a photo—
if he liked it he'd come visit-
And so he did.

We were married in 2003!

Laurin, 30

Easton....

I am a fashion designer and I have a crazy schedule. I am also a dreamer, I dream of a life in which I find my perfect other half. But that got me in a bad situation when my rush to find Mr. Right backfired on me.

I went on a trip to run away from my problems. At the time I was in an on-again/off-again relationship with my ex-boyfriend. I was confused about whether he was the one for me, or whether my best friend, who was also my partner in design, was a better match for me. I was convinced one of them was my soul mate. But which one? So I took a trip to clear my head.

I went to Cancun with a girlfriend and we started out the week partying like girls with no responsibilities! It was great. Tanning and relaxing...

The second day of the trip I met this guy and I instantly thought he was gay. We hit it off but the whole time while we were at the beach chatting and watching the sunrise I was thinking to myself "Too bad he is gay because he is soooo amazing." Turns out he wasn't gay and he started flirting with me. We had the best week and spent every moment together. By the end of the trip I had forgotten all of my man problems at home. Especially with this new person in my life who had already declared that I was the woman he was going to marry. That was the best thing to say to someone who believes so much that life can be a fairy tale.

The problem was that we were in two different cities. I was living in Montréal and he was from Toronto. For six months he swept me off my feet. He would come for the weekends with roses and would send me the sweetest e-mails. He was the most charming and patient man I had ever meant. We went to Turks and

Caicos where he proposed after six months of courtship. I said YES!!!

It all went crazy from that moment on. I still always wondered about the two guys I was confused about before I met him. However, I now realize that this was a form of escapism, and that's all it really was. We got married and I moved to Toronto and that is when I got to know the real him. He had brought me into his life but had no desire to be part of who I was. He was very cold and selfish and his Mom manipulated him in every way.

Our life was superficially beautiful. We had a nice house, two dogs, and we had great jobs. That being said, I was always the last priority on his list and we just didn't connect. He hurt me many times with his sharp tongue. Plus I travel a lot with my business and instead of taking advantage and meeting me for weekends in New York (or anywhere else I was) he decided to stay home and smoke pot. I loved him so much I took everything he did to me and accepted everything he took away from me. I tried to make it work. It was so hard to be away from my friends and my family.

Two years later and so much time lost. I realized that a marriage is not about thinking that everyday might be the last day, but that a husband should make you feel safe and protect you and care for you always. He was always able to turn against me and become a monster and a stranger. Sometimes I was truly scared of him.

I cried divorce one day when I couldn't take it anymore. I finally left. It wasn't the first time but this time it was for real.

I am back in Montréal now. The funny thing is that what I was trying to escape is still here and I am in the exact situation I was in before I left. The only difference is that now I am divorced. You can't escape who you are meant to be and some choices are really hard to make. I still don't know what choices to make.

Sometimes when something is so perfect you doubt it. I have the ultimate perfection in a relationship I have always had. He is my best friend and my partner in design. I am always with him and share so much with him. I grew up in his family and I admire him. People around us always say we are going to end up together. I guess you never know. He might be 'The One', or he might not. All I know is that I will never settle again. I will commit when I am fulfilled and until then I will keep searching for the answers.

The bottom line is that I still believe that life can be a fairy tale. Life can be whatever you want it to be. I have learned for the future, that's all.

Anonymous

Ethan....

I was in the beginning phases of a relationship, when I left the country to go to school in England. I was still really unclear as to what I wanted or if I even liked the guy. Sure, he seemed sweet enough. And don't we all want to be treated like a princess? In fact, he was the first person to show he cared by delivering flowers to me at work. Unfortunately for him, I was young and I didn't know what I wanted or how to graciously handle dating relationships. I thought guys were lame and romance made me uncomfortable. Not a good recipe for what was to transpire next.

I had been in school for about a month. I was having one of those days when you're wondering what your friends and family back home are up to. The mail came and, low and behold, there was a rather heavy parcel for me! How exciting!! By now I had almost forgotten about the guy I had left a million miles away in the grey-zone phase of a relationship.

The parcel was from him and I felt sick. I had decided that I didn't want to pursue anything and here was this package that couldn't have been cheap to send. I gingerly opened the parcel to find it full of dried rose petals with dried rosebuds lining the inside of the box. A letter was on top. In it he spelled out how he much missed me. This was a box that would have made any woman swoon, and here I was feeling like the Yorkshire pudding I had eaten for dinner was going to make a second appearance before high tea! I dug a little further into the box and found a big bag of Skittles, Pez, gum, pictures of himself with three of our other friends (two of whom were dating), and a CD I had been dying to buy! I was overwhelmed to say the least. I mean there were three dozen dried rosebuds, not to mention the dried rose petals, and then all the other goodies. It was a sweet gesture that was lost on a girl who didn't feel for him the way he felt for her.

By the time my overseas adventures had drawn to a close and I returned home, the romance was over and he had moved on. I was relieved to say the least. I was young and foolish, but I knew he wasn't the one for me. I just wasn't that into him.

He's now married to one of our mutual friends. Who could have known that the pictures in the box were symbolic of events to come? I was not in them, and now the other four people in the picture are married to one another.

Perhaps one day I'll get flowers again, except this time I'm ready for them!

Hollie, 24

Erik....

I decided to date the son of a man that I worked with. We spoke on the phone a lot and he invited me over to a party that he was attending in the same area that I lived in. He asked me if I did any skiing. I thought this was a strange question to ask since we were meeting in the fall, but I told him that, yes, I had done some skiing before but basically I "stick to the bunny hills."

When we met that night he introduced me to his mother who was also at the party happily bouncing on some man's lap and drunker than a skunk. And yes, the term skiing didn't mean skiing down a mountain - it meant the use of cocaine.

So I quickly left the party and never saw him again. But I had to laugh at myself for telling him that I only did bunny hills.

Danielle, 23

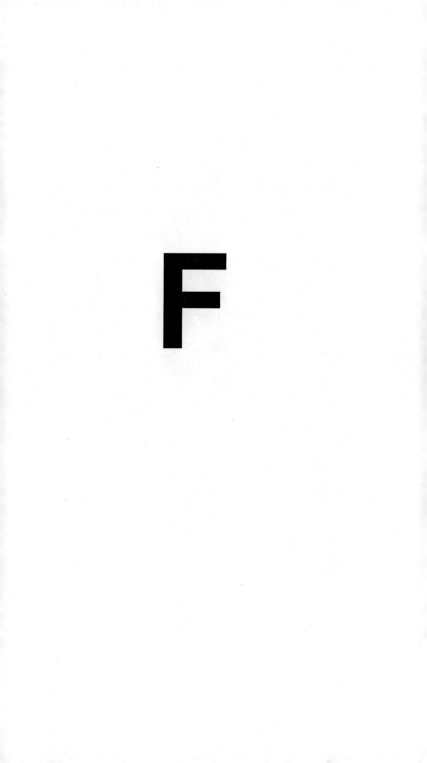

Fletcher....

I went out on a date with a bartender who worked at an established Halifax pub. We agreed to go to an Australian Wine Festival. I suggested we have dinner first, as this type of event on an empty stomach wouldn't be a good idea. He gallantly offered to 'spring' for dinner and took me out for cheap greasy pub food.

While mingling at the event he graciously introduced me to a woman he used to work with. Upon her departure he informed me he hadn't seen her in several years. However, he hoped she was "better in bed now than she was then."

Adequate beer slinger? Maybe. Class? None.

Shelagh, 28

Fraser....

I was 18 and he was my first boyfriend. After a wonderful dinner, we walked back to his car. He opened my door, and in my seat sat a beautiful teddy bear. It was holding a single red rose and a heart-shaped box of chocolates!

I turned around and gave him a huge hug, a kiss, and told him how much I loved the presents.

We have since broken up but we remain friends. I still have that teddy bear. Every time I look at it I am reminded of him and the good times we had.

Christina, 21

Frank....

I had just moved to a new city and there was a play coming through that I really wanted to see. A new friend of mine mentioned that an "older man" she knew through work had tickets and was looking for someone to take. Not wanting it to be awkward or have the wrong expectations placed on the night, I told her I wasn't interested. A couple of days later Frank called me and told me that there was no pressure and that he needed someone to go to this work function with him. He made it clear that there were no ulterior motives. So, I went. He was very pleasant. At 39, he was closer in age to my father than to me, but I tried not to think about that. Throughout the night he was a total gentleman and there was no awkwardness between us. After that night we exchanged emails and once in a while he sent me information on things going on in the city to keep me up to date as I was still so new to Toronto.

A couple of months after I met him he emailed me telling me he had tickets to a sporting event. He asked if I wanted to go since I had never been to see a live sports game. I thought it sounded like fun so I went.

The entire night was a disaster. This time, from the moment I saw him it was different. He always had his hand on my back or was trying to be in contact of some sort. Whenever he introduced me to his work colleagues, he made no effort to correct them when they assumed we were together. I ended up spending the entire night trying to avoid him, not knowing anyone else in the box, and not enjoying the game at all.

About halfway through the night I met a woman who was there with one of Frank's colleagues. We started chatting and connected on a professional and personal level and exchanged business cards.

Later that night, when the game was over I drove Frank to his car and thanked him for the night out. He leaned over and tried to kiss me. I pushed him away and told him that I was not interested in that type of a relationship at all, as I had made clear over and over again. He looked at me and said, "What, I give you two expensive tickets and you can't even kiss me?" At that point I told Frank to get out of my car immediately. I haven't talked to him since.

About six months later the woman I met that night and I arranged to meet for lunch. As we chatted it came out that we had rescued each other. It turns out her partner, whom she had just recently separated from, had asked her to come to the event with him so he wouldn't have to explain the separation to his colleagues. Throughout the entire evening she had felt pressured and awkward. She said that talking to me for most of the night had saved her. Looking back on it now, we both laugh – but that night I don't think either of us were laughing! Frank turned out to be a jerk, but at least I made a new friend out of the deal.

Irene, 23

Gerry....

I was the girl who didn't really have a boyfriend in school (we're talking from kindergarten to grade twelve). If by some miracle I did have a boyfriend it would always end before the big three-month goal. I was very set in my ways and I would never ask a boy out (that was their job). If a boy did pay attention to me I automatically fell in love. It didn't matter if we had anything in common, or if there was any chemistry between us, I wanted a boyfriend and I was willing to try to make anything work.

That brings us to about four years ago. I had just started a new job. I didn't know what I wanted to do with my life, and I was extremely discouraged by the whole dating scene. Most of my friends were married or in long-term relationships. I felt alone. That's when I met Gerry. We met through mutual friends at work. It wasn't an immediate attraction (he's absolutely nothing like any of the other guys I've dated) but the more we saw each other, the more we talked, the more I found myself falling for him. He made me laugh and feel good about myself. And the best part was, he wasn't smooth at all – he was just as clumsy and awkward as myself. But nothing happened! He never called, and he never asked me out. I couldn't figure it out.

A few months went by, and still nothing. A Christmas party that we would both be attending was coming up, and I wanted to go with Gerry. He didn't ask me to go with him, so I went with someone else. I was having a pretty good time, but Gerry was on my mind all night. So finally, near the end of the evening I asked him to dance. I wasn't quite sure what I was going to say but I had had enough of this game we were playing. As soon as we got onto the dance floor I started to tell him off. I said that I didn't know why he hadn't called, but I did know that if he didn't call me sometime tomorrow, I wasn't going to waste any more of my energy thinking about him and that he would have lost his chance with me. Pretty ballsy move right? Well it worked! He called the next day. We had our first date on the 21st of December and have been together every day since then. We are now engaged and have plans to marry next year.

The moral of this story is: when the time is right, it'll happen. You can't rush fate. And if it's right, you can't mess it up.

Denise, 24

Grant....

When I was 19 I was out with a girlfriend and through the smoke filled room I spotted a man that took my breath away. I then turned to tell my friend, pointing at this stranger, that one day I would marry him. She looked at me as if I had lost my mind. His friend came up to me and insisted that I had to meet his friend that was trying to get enough nerve to come up to me all night. In the back of my mind I was hoping it was 'The One'. I turned around, and it was him! Full of excitement we started to talk and hit it off right away. The next day he actually called not once but four times. Little did I know this would be the start of a seven-and-a-half year relationship that would scar me in ways I couldn't have imagined.

Grant and I started to see each other immediately. I was in my second year of college and he was no longer in school. I had always been the carefree girl who literally lived life to its fullest. This trait of mine started to deteriorate as time went on. We dated on and off for the first two years. I grew up in Niagara Falls so I was unaware of his friends or his past. He seemed to always try to control me, and as I look back now it is more obvious to me. There were a lot of fights and not speaking with one another, but I always used the excuse that we were young and that he was right for me and a good person inside. Finally after about two-and-a-half years I had had enough and decided that if I wanted to make a life for myself I had to let him go – and that is what I did. I blocked out his phone number so he could not reach me and stayed away from places I knew he would be.

One day he saw a friend of mine and expressed how he would do anything to have me back. She phoned me and he came on the phone and that was all it took for me to take him back. We met each other's families and became one. I moved back to Niagara Falls. He stayed in Toronto and we had a long distance relationship. We would see each other on weekends. Finally eight months later I moved and rented an apartment in Mississauga. He was very excited.

I worked two jobs to pay the rent and bills while he sat on the couch growing larger. He started to become very jealous and controlling. I got fired from two jobs because he would show up there and fight with me. He put down some rules which included that I was not to go out anywhere with my friends and I was to listen to him because he was the man and that was all there was to it. I broke it off with him and he would sit outside my apartment and watch me, call my parents, and try to cause a disaster.

After about two months he showed up again screaming my name from under my window. I had a coffee with him. I felt sorry for him and I decided to give it another chance. It took me three months to conjure up any kind of feeling for him. I was not happy, but I stayed and thought it would get better. I told him he had to start helping with the rent and he decided that it was time for me to move back to Niagara Falls so we could save for a house. I agreed and went back and commuted every day to Mississauga. Around this time SARS had an outbreak in Toronto and he had a safety business so we dedicated three weeks in pushing for sales. The business was amazing. Once he made that money he changed and did not want to be with me anymore. I was devastated. He closed his business and ran with the money. He did not pay any of his suppliers. He moved to Kingston to run a restaurant and left me in the dark. I wanted to die. My whole world came crashing down on me. The only guy I had ever known and loved had left me with no explanation. I found out he had been cheating on me as well. I also still worked for his brother.

As time went on I became okay. I met a wonderful man who knew how to treat a lady and I tried to make it work with him, but I was not ready so I had to end it with him. I stayed single for eight months, bought a house with my best friend, and I finally felt I was on the right path. I had heard that Grant missed me and wanted me back and I thought no way in hell! Then one day he came into my work and for some reason I took him back immediately.

The first two months were amazing – it was like he was an angel, my angel. I ended up leaving my job and had a really hard time finding another one. He proposed to me after being together for two-and-a-half months. I remember this like it was yesterday. I was in New York with my friend and I found out he had bought me a ring. I started to cry. I knew it was too soon. When I got back from New York I sat on my porch with my best friend and let her know my feelings. She said that if he did propose I should just go with what my heart told me to do, and that is what I did.

He proposed in Niagara on the Lake and planned out the perfect day and night for us. I felt like a princess, his princess, and I accepted. The next day my mother had a party at her house and his family was there too. I felt ashamed in front of everyone and was not completely content.

Two months later his mother started to cause problems for us and I started to think, "If I married him, I will have to deal with his mother for the rest of my life!" He started to mentally and verbally abuse me and we were fighting like cats and dogs. I could not let my family know because I forced them to accept him again and I was very embarrassed. This went on for six months. Sometimes he would disappear for one week and not call. I had no self-esteem left and sometimes I actually hated him. He constantly told me how miserable I was and always put me down. I started to believe him and I started to believe without him I would not make it. I cried myself to sleep almost every night and I prayed to God that he would guide me in the right direction. I knew that this person (who thought he was a man) was slowly killing me inside.

We went to Niagara Falls for our marriage class and got into an embarrassing fight in front of my parents. He proceeded to say that I was miserable and crazy and that he would change me once we were married. My parents begged him to let me go. He said he never could and he never would. The next day we went to our marriage classes and I knew it was over. I felt ashamed to be there and he finally disgusted me. We drove back to Toronto and I stepped out of his car, said goodbye, and walked away for good.

I walked into my house and packed all his stuff (even the fake cheap jewelry that his mother gave me) and the next day I just left it on his porch for him to find. I called everyone in the wedding party and let them know it was over and I was canceling the wedding. I sent out an email to everyone I knew. I have never spoken to him again. I walked away and everyday I gain more strength and self-esteem.

Since I left him the police have told him to stay away from me. To this day I don't know if he will leave me alone in the future. It is a risk I took and am willing to take to get my life back. I thank God, my friends, and my family for all of the support they gave me. I am happier now then ever before.

Now I will never settle and will only look at the positive aspects of life. I could have been married right now and he would have abused me and cheated on me and I would have had to work three jobs to support us. I know that he will be punished for all his actions. Everything comes back to haunt you one day. For myself, looking at my life over the last eight years, I now know that there are so many women out there who have never really dated. They only know one partner and they will stick with that one person even if they know that person is no good for them. It is the hardest thing in my life that I have ever gone through. But each day I know it will get better because I gain strength. I am learning who I am for the first time in a long time...

Linda, 27

Guy....

How do you decide whether a person is right for you in terms of future commitment? You cannot tell on the first date, and even on the first few dates. But women should think about the man's relationship with his mother.

This is a story of my first marriage.

We were both rather young, I was 21 and he was 22. He had just finished university and started working while I was still in my last year. I met his parents rather early on into our relationship, but it was mostly for polite family dinners where I could not really tell how dependent my future fiancé was on his mother. She turned out to be a very dominant woman who was ruling her gentle husband and their only son.

When we got married I imagined we would eventually rent a place of our own, but in the meantime we would live in my parents' mostly vacant cottage in the spring and summer while we looked for a city place to rent in the fall. Thank goodness there was no phone at the cottage so my mother-in-law could not call us all the time. However, she started calling my new husband at his work every day.

One morning we were lazing around in bed (we were still newlyweds) and my husband decided to go into work at a later time. I did not think it was a big deal. He left and I stayed at the cottage, sun-tanning and reading up for my final exams. All of a sudden a taxi arrived. Turns out my mother-in-law had rung her only son at work, he was not there, and she thought, "Something happened!" She had hired a taxi and rushed all the way from the city to check on him at the cottage. I was shocked and tried hard to mumble excuses as to why her darling was not at work.

Another time, we both came back to the cottage to find out that she had visited the cabin – without us. She had found the spare key by the door and cleaned everything inside. She rearranged the food in the fridge, cooked, brought some food, and even went through all our personal clothes and other belongings in the wardrobe and dresser, folding it all into neater piles – more to her liking. I was shocked! This was a horrible invasion of privacy! But again, I did not want to be rude and confront the older woman. Besides, when we returned that day, she was gone. She had performed the "good deed" and disappeared.

Silver Lining

When the summer was over and we still had not found a place to rent (my husband was hardly looking), my mother-in-law announced that she could not imagine living without her son and suggested that we should live one week with them (I protested) and one week with my parents, and alternate like some teenagers having a sleep-over! It never got that far.

The final straw happened when we were back in the city. I suddenly had a back pain attack and had to be hospitalized on a stretcher because I could not move. My husband had a slight cold at the time and my mother-in-law had been checking on him frequently.

When the ambulance dropped me off in the ER the attendants abandoned me in a dark room next to a dying, moaning, and vomiting old woman. I was in so much pain and horrified of my surroundings. All I wanted was some support, someone to go find the doctor, or someone to take charge and to wheel me out of there, back into a car and get me home. My husband with his light sniffles was sitting in the chair by the wall worrying that if his mother called him at that moment and discovered he had left home while being under the weather, he would be in trouble! This may have been the time when I finally realized I had definitely made a huge mistake by marrying that 6'5" creature in the chair.

Luckily, it did not last long. We separated after less than two months of "marital bliss." He moved back in with his parents and later sent his daddy to pick up his belongings that I had gladly piled up in a bunch of bags! The only time I ever saw the mommy's boy after that was when we had to meet at city hall to sign the final divorce papers. Later that evening I threw a great "Divorce Party" with my friends and my new boyfriend, my divorce certificate proudly pinned to the wall in the main room! It sounds like a fun ending, and it was, but the whole experience of such a pathetic first marriage was really not something I'd wish on anyone.

They say the way a man treats his mother is how he will eventually treat you as his wife. But enough is enough and every woman should try to find out about her mother-in-law ahead of time.

Anonymous, 38

Haden....

One night my friend and I went out to meet some friends. I met Haden at the bar we went to. In a group of hundreds of people, Haden and I somehow started talking – and talked for the better part of an hour. His friends were moving downstairs to the bar beneath our current location and he made me promise that I would come down there soon. I agreed but when I went down to the other bar there was a long line up and my friends wanted to leave. Though really disappointed, I didn't want to be 'that girl' who made her friends wait in line forever for some guy she had only talked to for an hour. So we left.

The next day I was on campus and I saw Haden across one of the walkways from me. All of a sudden I felt shy and weird and I turned the other way before he saw me! About a month later I was on a road trip with one of my best friends and a friend of hers who I had just met that weekend. As we were driving home, out of the blue, my friend's friend turned off the music, turned into the back seat with this extremely excited look on her face and said "Oh my god, Sabrina. I just realized that I know the PERFECT guy for you!" I just laughed and told her that I didn't want to be set up. She told she would leave me alone as soon as she told me all about him. As she started describing him it sounded more and more like Haden. Finally, I asked what his name was – and sure enough – it was Haden. I told her that I had met Haden, that I liked him, and thought that maybe he had been interested in me too. She was ecstatic – but I made her promise she wouldn't tell him about our conversation in case I looked like a stalker.

A month later I got a call from her. She told me she had run into Haden's best friend and mentioned my name. Haden's friend remembered that I was the girl who "hadn't come downstairs." Apparently Haden had been as disappointed as I had been. Even at this point I didn't want to push things so again I made her promise that she wouldn't act on anything.

At the end of August I got called to Vancouver for work. My staff and I flew to Vancouver early Monday morning and flew home that same Monday night. We had a stopover in Kelowna. About half way to Kelowna the stewardess came up to me to tell me that they had double booked my seat and that I would have to change seats for the flight from Kelowna to Edmonton. I had a group booking with my staff, I was tired, and it didn't make sense to me. Why wouldn't they put the other person who would be boarding in Kelowna into a new seat? I fought with the stewardess for a bit, finally giving up and moving to my new seat. The two seats beside me were empty after the plane had boarded so I was looking forward to stretching out and taking a nap. At the very last minute a late passenger boarded and sat beside me. As he got settled into his seat, I didn't even look up. I was reading a book and I was so tired that conversation was the last thing I wanted. He kept trying to start a conversation with me but I would have none of it. Finally I quit being so stubborn and we started chatting. About twenty minutes into the conversation he started to look and feel more and more familiar. Finally, he introduced himself as Haden. I just about fell out of my seat! I shook his hand and told him that my name was Sabrina. I could see him process the information and the same shock come over him. Before we got off the plane he told me that he wouldn't risk losing me twice before getting my number. He called me the next day and our first date was two days later.

Our connection was instantaneous and incredibly strong. Our first date was twenty-one hours long. The next day he met my family and within two weeks his parents flew in to meet me. Five weeks into our intense relationship we got word that he had been transferred out east. I had two years of university left and he had no definite plans to be back out west. With the decision looming to either date long distance (with no visible end in sight), or leave the relationship behind, we went through an incredibly stressful decision time that ultimately resulted in us alienating ourselves from each other because we couldn't decide what to do or how to handle the situation. Although, in the end, we handled the situation poorly, the whole relationship confirmed my belief that everything happens for a reason. People come in and out of your life for a reason. Clearly Haden was meant to be a part of my life – there were too many indications for that to not be true. Our time together was short and sweet but in every relationship you learn just a bit more about yourself. I learnt that fate and thinking you care about someone is not enough. Haden and I came to a crossroads, and even though we both said we really wanted to be together, we didn't want to sacrifice anything for that to be true. You can fall in love, but you have to make the decision to put the work into the relationship – so you stay in love.

Sabrina, 34

Hugh....

I am 66-years-old and single, although I have been married twice before. I met my soul mate last year on the Internet. We met through a dating service and soon we were chatting every night on one of the chat lines. We had a web cam so we could see each other, and he was a charming and good-looking man. It soon became apparent that we had a lot in common. After two weeks we decided to get together and I made a train trip of more then seven hours to meet him. He paid for the train fare and he was waiting for me at the train station with a large bouquet of roses.

He was as charming in real life as he had been on the net. He was not pushy in any way. He even gave me the choice as to where I wanted to sleep, as I was to stay for about four days at his home. We talked a lot, he showed me around his home, and introduced me to his hobby of model railroading which was also his business. He was an absolute gentleman, and I was completely in love with this man. He told me many times over that he was absolutely taken with me as well. We had so much in common, and we both marveled at that.

After four days, I took the trip home again, but we stayed in touch by phone and the Internet. He decided to make the long trip the next month by car to see me. He was getting cold feet by November, but he had a host of excuses to explain it. The best excuse, to my way of thinking, was that he was not used to having a woman in his life as he had been alone for more than two years. He changed his mind about spending time together in December around Christmas, and cancelled my visit (although we had a few days together at my place earlier in the month). So I decided to go down again to his place on the train in January, but he cancelled that too. That was when I got suspicious, but he assured me that nothing was wrong and that I worried too much. He promised to come and see me in February.

In the meantime, I was not able to get him online every night and he did not answer my phone calls. Then I found him online on a dating website and I had a light bulb moment. He had forwarded a joke to me, and attached to it was the email address of a lady that he had told me was a family friend. I decided to write this lady a letter. My suspicions were proved correct, as she was a lady he was also seeing while he was seeing me. This devastated her, as she had absolutely no idea that he was seeing me too. This lady found some email addresses in her files of letters and I decided to track them down. By that time, it did not surprise me to discover that he had a host of women on the net that he had gone to see. One of the women even lived out West. He was the biggest liar I had ever met and a master of deceit.

I confronted him on the phone about all of this, but he outright told me he had done nothing wrong. I also spoke to his daughter, whom I had met on several occasions, and she finally confided in me that he had cheated on their mother when she was alive. His daughter told me that he loves to be dramatic and constantly needs attention from someone, be it on the net or otherwise. She had high hopes after meeting me that I would be the one to stay with her dad and that things would be 'normal' from then on.

Needless to say, this experience has left me with a very bitter taste in my mouth. I think this man is a very sick person – for him it is all about the hunt, and to see how far he can go and what he can get away with. I managed to get him kicked out of quite a few dating services because they are all interconnected through relationship exchange. Once your name is on one, you are on all of them.

As a result of this experience, dating anyone is now a bit of a hit and miss. I am very cautious before agreeing to a relationship. I ask a lot of questions, and some men are put off by this, but I figure if you have nothing to hide why not answer the questions? Myself, I am up front about who I am and what I would like in a relationship, and I am truthful about my past. That way I have no regrets, and I do not have to lie to keep the truth from coming out. Lies always catch up with you in the end, but it seems a lot of people don't know that.

My advice for women is to be very careful. Don't ignore the red flags that go up when you meet someone. Those red flags are warnings that cannot be ignored. These things are usually quite obvious when you meet someone for the first time, and even more so the second time around. After that, it's time to say, "No, thank you. I don't think we are a match." There is no need to offer any explanation, but I always say that "we are not a match" if I am asked.

Soulmates, 66

Hank....

I've had a few dates that rank right up there with the world's worst. However, the real winner was with a cowboy I met who seemed very gentlemanly and polite. He took me to dinner at a nice seafood restaurant.

The server asked him if he wanted a drink, and he proceeded to tell his whole life story as to why he would love a drink, but couldn't have one. The server finally looked at me for help as I ordered him a 7Up and myself a coffee.

He then ordered us both the fish and chips because it was the special, without asking me. I don't eat fried fish and I don't like chips. When dinner arrived he picked up his fish with his fingers and proceeded to eat it. At no point during the entire meal did he pick up his knife and fork. He even reached over the table to eat the discarded fish batter and chips off my plate with his fingers.

He also decided that he liked some music that was playing. We were sitting by the front window and the server was as far from us as possible at the back of the restaurant. Rather than wait to swallow his mouthful of food and wait for the server to come to us, he proceeded to holler the length of the restaurant wanting to know what CD they were playing.

Conversation during dinner consisted of him bursting into song lyrics when he had no response to something I had said, or when there was lull in conversation. When dinner was over he walked me to my truck berating me the entire time for buying a standard transmission truck because women should drive small automatic cars. He turned out to be a knuckle dragger if I ever met one. Needless to say, it was our first date, and our last.

Anonymous

Ian....

I stare at you with tears in my eyes. You know I'd come with you if I could, you say. I'm so sorry, you say.

The anxiousness in my stomach about what lies ahead for me. Knowing that I have to hold it together and be strong.

This death is so messy. It's messy.

So many unresolved feelings. So many secrets and conversations left unsaid. I am scared. I am sad. I need you to hold me tight and not let go.

Stay with me tonight, I ask.

Okay, you reply.

I need you tonight, I say.

Okay, you reply.

That night you stay with me.

The next day, packing to leave. Preparing to see my Mom, my Aunt, and my Grandma. My dear Grandmamma whose own heartbreak after losing her husband of 65 years has left her lost, confused, and broken. She is in denial. Denying his death. Denying that what she has lived for all these years is finally gone. We are saddened. We are relieved. The man that has shrouded our family in fear and silence is finally dead. We are free. Free from his oppression, his violence.

Can you stay with me one last night, I ask.

Silver Lining

I am scared. I am sad.
A deeply entrenched sadness suddenly washes over me.

I am angry. Mourning the grandfather I never had, the grandfather I wish I could have had.

You start. You had plans tonight.

I start.

The realization that you do not want to be there for me hits me like a tidal wave drowning out any reason. I cannot believe your response.

I would be there for you if someone in your family died, I yell.

I wouldn't want you to be, you retort. I'd want to be by myself.

Well, I don't, I sob.

In the end you regress. That night you hug me. You kiss me.

I love you, you say.

I love you too, I say.

I say it. But I am confused. There is hollowness to our words.

How do you do it, I wonder. How do you gloss over everything?

I am sad! I want to scream it at you in the darkness. Break down that wall between us.

I am silent.

94

You stay with me until I depart early the next morning.

I stare out the window of the bus.
I am scared for what is ahead of me, but strong.
I am an adult now.
I am going to be with my family.
I am going to be there for my family.

I am in control, of my life, of my happiness.

Like death, sudden and out of my control, I realize that you do not make me happy. I love you passionately, but you are unable to give me what I need at one of the most crucial times of my life. Are you scared? Are you selfish? How is it that you lack empathy for a person that you claim to love?

I cannot reconcile your words, your touch, with your actions.

I wait two months until I break up with you. Three more months after that I stop guessing, stop caring, about why you weren't there for me that day.

Still loving you. Knowing you're not good for me.

Knowing I need a man, not a boy.

Still loving you...

With these words, I let go.

Sarah, 24

Ivan....

After having dated too many boys, I was tired of meeting idiots, and I was tired of being let down.

I had just moved back home after spending some time in another city. I was still settling, and I was in no mood to meet anyone serious. One Saturday night my friend Linda invited me to a bar, the sleaziest meat-market club in Edmonton. True, I was a party girl, but I hated the scene at this bar! However, I hadn't seen Linda in ages, so I went. I turned out to be the only sober person in the group, and Linda was the only one I knew. She and some girls decided to go hit the dance floor. I reluctantly went along so I wouldn't have to be left with drunken strangers.

After a few minutes, I noticed Tony, an old friend from university, standing on the edge of the dance floor. I also noticed that he was with a group of tall boys - my favorite! I told Linda I'd be back.

Once I got to Tony I no longer saw a group of boys, I saw only Ivan. He was gorgeous. His smile melted me. Eventually, after my protestations (I was wearing my glasses, my hair in a ponytail, and I had forgotten a belt) Tony introduced us. I was dumbfounded.

Usually confident, I literally looked down at my shoes because I didn't know what to say to this beautiful guy. He talked to me and we hit it off! We got along great and even exchanged phone numbers. The down side - he lived 1200 kilometres away. He also had a girlfriend.

Despite all of this, I called him the next day. I figured that at the very least he might provide a little action when he came back to town. Little did I know the impression I had left on him. He had been excited by our conversations. He even thought I was gorgeous, despite my thoughts on the subject.

He broke up with his girlfriend two days after we met. We have spoken every single day since. It has been a year-and-a-half and we are as in love as the moment we met.

Who knew a girl could meet the man of her dreams in Edmonton's biggest meat-market?

Lerina, 24

Imad....

The fact that we even met is amazing. Every little detail had to be perfect to orchestrate our meeting.

I had to be in Europe. I had to have run out of money and be heading back to catch an early flight home. I had to have decided to take the Chunnel from Paris to London, instead of flying like I originally planned. It was important that I couldn't get on the earlier Chunnel, as frustrating as it was, and had to buy a ticket that fateful morning. I had to get lost on the way to the train station to time it right. And I had to be unsure of where I was supposed to buy a ticket, unsure enough to ask him for help.

If that hadn't happened I wouldn't have been behind Imad in the queue to buy my train ticket. The fact that he spoke English, albeit not fluently, was amazing. The fact that he was cute added to it all.

I remember that the first thing he did was laugh at me and tell me to calm down. I must have looked like a wreck. I hadn't showered that morning at the hostel and I was wearing an extremely harried expression with not one splotch of make-up.

After assuring me that I was in the right queue, and assuring me that I would get on my train, we started to chat. He was taking a train somewhere for work. Where, I don't know. At that moment I wasn't really paying attention to him. All I could do was continue to panic about getting on that train. If I missed it, I would miss my plane in London that would take me to Edinburgh.

He sensed my panic and let me in front of him in the line-up even though he was in more of a hurry than me. His train left in an hour, mine in five.

I don't recall our conversation. I do remember that he teased me and laughed a lot. He had a good laugh, deep and true. And he was wearing a suit so he apparently had a good job. Hey, I'm not completely blind.

When we got to the window he helped me explain to the ticket agent what I needed. And of course, as luck would have it, I couldn't get on the right Chunnel and had to take the one an hour later. (That's another story but I did make it to my plane).

Anyhow, that gave me one more thing to think about and I still failed to notice Imad properly. Which, if you knew me, and I guess you don't, you would be absolutely flabbergasted that I didn't notice a cute boy. I am kind of a connoisseur of cute boys.

Luckily for me, he apparently thought I was cute enough to ask me to have a coffee before his train left. Unluckily for me, I'm idiotic and said no because I had to get back to the hostel. Once again he was the smarter of the two of us and at least asked me for my email address.

So that was it. I didn't even think about him again until I was home in Canada and received an email from him. Since then we've been chatting online at least twice a week, through which I learned that he is an engineer, rich, single, speaks four languages, and is even of the same faith as me. He is also hilarious, intelligent, and just quirky enough to be interesting. He told me that he is tired of the dating scene and wants to be with one girl who has the same travel bug that he does. (Once again, if you knew me you would know that this is exactly what I've been waiting for a guy to say for years).

Imad also told me via the Internet that he fell for me the moment that I smiled.

Too bad he lives in Paris.

Erika, 22

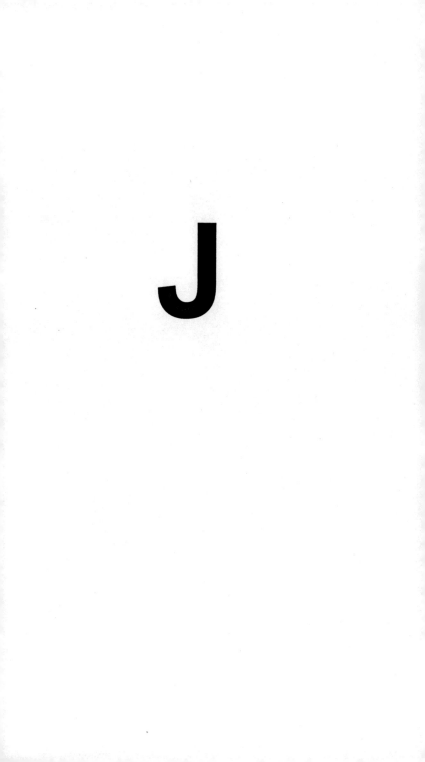

J

Jesse....

Jesse gave me apple butter as a gift – on our first date – because he thought I would be the kind of girl who liked apples. What?!

Carissa, 23

Juan....

During my twenties, I went on one or two dates a week. I never went into the dates thinking 'relationship', and thus, I always had fun. My mother always said, "Go out with him, you never know who else you're going to meet."

Here's one dating story for you...

I was heavily into learning how to Salsa. Toronto was a hot spot for this and I was going to clubs that hosted primarily Latino men. I loved the music and felt it was a great way to learn something new while exercising. It was also a great way to meet people.

The men were so wonderful and passionate about the music that they would sing to me as we danced several songs in a row. One man stands out - Juan. After a few months of hanging out at the club he asked me out on a date. He was a lot of fun, as well as a smooth and gentle dancer, so I figured dating him would result in a similar experience.

The night of our date I drove to his apartment on College Street (in downtown Toronto), and knocked on his door. Juan opened the door and gave me a bear hug. He then ran back into the kitchen, popped down a vile of ginseng, and proceeded to play his flute.

Silver Lining

Later he decided we should go out, but first we had to drop off his car at a stereo installation place. I followed him in my car. So much for our funky night out on College Street!

We drove for at least a half hour to get to the stereo installation place. Juan dropped his car off and finally, all excited, he hopped into my car and told me to drive, all the while giving me directions. We ended up in North Toronto.

So far the fun I had been expecting hadn't happened. We pulled into a subdivision at which point I asked him to clarify where we were going. To my surprise he replied that we were at his mother's house, just as we were turning into the driveway. In a slight state of shock as well as curiosity, I followed him in. There was his whole family sitting in the kitchen, including his sister who was in her housecoat and two weeks overdue in her pregnancy.

They welcomed me to sit down, so I did. His mom turned on the stove and out came the frying pan, oil, eggs, and rice. Within ten minutes I was eating a lot of food. Juan wolfed down a plate of food without so much as a word to anyone while I was trying to eat politely and answer questions from his family, which is a little difficult with your mouth full of rice.

He got up from the table, kissed his mom and thanked her (admittedly endearing), and ran upstairs to his old bedroom leaving me with the family. At first I was a little nervous, but because this had never happened to me on a first date, I was rather intrigued and thought it would be one of those one-of-a-kind stories I would tell later. I ended up having a great time chatting with his family.

An hour later I heard bongo drums from upstairs. The sound continued for a while before Juan decided to bring the drums downstairs. We left shortly after that and I drove him and his drums back home downtown. He invited me in and I thought this would be a great idea, since I had hardly talked to him all night. Apparently he thought we had talked enough and started getting really touchy, so I declined his services and left promptly. I must have laughed most of the ride home.

I still danced once in awhile with Juan but I never went out with him or anyone else from the club again. I am married now and living in Alberta with a little one on the way. I still love to salsa and so does my husband, however he is neither smooth nor passionate about it, and that suits me just fine.

Jess, 32

Jason....

My story comes straight out of a fun-filled first year of university. Having ended a long-term relationship with a controlling, possessive type around Thanksgiving of first-year, I enjoyed my free time and wasn't looking for anything more than fun. Ok, so this is another one of those love-finds-you-when-you-least-expect-it stories, but there's complications, and that's where the lessons come from, so don't quit reading yet. It's also proof you can meet people worth dating at the bar.

I met Jason at 'The Zoo', a bar in my hometown of North Bay, ON, about a month after returning from my first-year at school. I sat on his lap and flirted with him until after closing time. We went back to his place, where I was sick from too much beer, and we slept beside each other all night. He didn't try to take advantage of my beer-filled state, always the sign of a good guy.

105

Silver Lining

For the next couple of weeks we would make plans and occasionally run into each other. We quickly became inseparable. My mom knew I was in love before I did. Complete strangers apparently had the same impression. People stopped us more than once that summer to tell us how much love we radiated together. We eventually confessed our love for each other (he told me the first time by signing it into my back while we lay in bed) despite knowing each other such a short time. Aw, sweet, right? Well it was, for almost three months.

I had to go back to Mississauga for school in September. He helped move me down, and then moved down himself in October after fixing up a used truck. I don't think the residence office at my university knows he lived with me on campus until Christmas break, but whatever. After trouble finding suitable employment, and his truck breaking down beyond repair, and getting a planter's wart so bad it needed surgery to be removed, Jay decided to stay in North Bay after Christmas while I returned to Mississauga.

Sometimes five or six weeks would go by during which all we'd have of each other was a voice 400 kilometres away. He'd come visit, but I'd be busy with school, and I would feel badly that we didn't get to spend as much quality time together as we wanted. Or I'd ignore my school work and then feel super-stressed to get it all done after he left. Sometimes I had to remind myself to behave, that my fun-filled year before may have been easier, but it didn't mean as much to me as this wonderful man and the love we shared. It was a lot of tears and long-distance phone bills.

During the summer, I returned to North Bay and we shared an apartment. We were together again. Smooth sailing now, right? I can hear everyone who's ever lived with their lover laughing right now at my naïveté. After some time we found summer jobs we loved but they had totally different schedules. Jason was trailblazing for the Eco Park three days a week, often wanting to party it up with his co-worker and cousin upon return. I worked five days a week writing and couldn't deal with the late nights they brought home on weekdays. We argued about partying, money and guests but managed to hold it together. Barely.

The following September we both returned to school. Jason went to Lindsay, to Sir Sanford Fleming for environmental technology. He was closer to my Mississauga campus, but still far away. We managed to see each other every two or three weeks and we continued to talk a lot on the phone. But we'd still argue, especially about partying ("Where were you when I called?"), why he wouldn't call when he said he would (I've come to realize the not-phoning is, for the most part, just a guy thing), and whether we should stay together through all this. More tears, more long-distance phone bills, more nights waiting up for the phone to ring.

Having been promised a return to my writing job in June, we took May to go out to British Columbia by bus, a grueling though worthwhile adventure. Getting back to North Bay with no remaining funds, we returned and looked for work. I got word that the HRDC funding for my writing job was not granted and eventually found a minimum wage job sanding and painting someone's deck. Jason got on at a local gallery, but with part-time hours. We had more money arguments (they always seem so foolish yet important at the same time), more partying arguments, more something-isn't-working arguments...and then, an infidelity. Drunken though it was, it was heart-wrenchingly painful for us both. Where do we go from here? Do we throw in the towel now because of one mistake? How do we get past this? Time. So much time that when we both returned to school in September, we declared we were on a break.

What does 'a break' mean? I still don't know. It's not like we were really broken up; we still visited every few weeks and talked often on the phone. But something was different. A distance had come between us, something less tangible but harder-hitting than the physical distance imposed by our scholarly pursuits. After being approached by suitors within the first month or so back at school, I came to realize I didn't want to date anyone else. Jason came to the same realization, perhaps partly through my sharing suitor stories, perhaps not. However, knowing you don't want to be with anyone else doesn't make everything alright. It doesn't mean being together is easy. The dilemma of working through our problems remained, particularly because long-distance is a hard way to resolve relationship issues.

We kept at it through that year. We spent another summer together and another school year apart. We often questioned whether the hardships were worth it, especially when we hadn't seen each other in over a month or had our third argument that week. Something held us to each other, some connection that clicked when we met over four years ago and was able to travel the distance between us, physical and emotional. We've definitely worked out many of our issues through open and honest communication. It's the best relationship tool ever! But, like with any couple, there are always things coming up between us that need to be resolved. How will we know if we can work through them all and build a life as partners? Time. Time together.

Johanna, 24

Jon....

Jon was a nice guy, a good and solid guy, a guy with confidence and self-esteem. In retrospect, Jon was a guy I probably should have given a better opportunity to. But I didn't and I am embarrassed to say why. He was... well, just not as cute as the other guys I had been with. He was short. He had a small belly and a goofy face. But I was attracted to his confidence and decided to give the relationship a chance.

I never introduced him to any of my friends, which in hindsight should have been a sign to me. Although we were together for more than three months I never felt tempted to have sex with him. I told him I wanted to wait, but the fact was it proved easy to wait, which also should have told me something. Plus, he was a sloppy kisser and I figure if a guy can't kiss, he probably won't be any good at other intimate acts. But he really was a nice guy and I still feel bad when I think about how I couldn't get beyond his looks. Especially since I've always told myself that beauty is only skin-deep and that it's what's inside that matters. I guess it's easier to believe that in theory rather than in practice. I'd like to hope that if I met another 'Jon' today I'd be able to look beyond the exterior.

But I've got to admit that bad kissing would still be a deal breaker for me.

Kathryn, 32

Jack....

I have been in relationships before and I have been married. I am now divorced with children. However, I truly believe that God works in mysterious ways.

109

Silver Lining

Otherwise, I would not have met Jack.

I think I was turning into one of those cynical women who didn't believe that love existed. Even the thought of true love or discussions about 'soul mates' would make me gag. Well, with that said, this is my story...

I went out with a few friends one night, and it ended very abruptly. Let's just say that some people should drink, and some shouldn't bother. Anyways, it was still early and I didn't want to go home and Jack's name came to mind. At first I thought, "No I can't go there." But somehow I ended up at his house and we talked until the sun came up. We had known each other for years, but that night I felt as if I had known him all my life.

In June 2004 he called to ask me out on a date for the coming weekend. I said, yes. Unknowingly I would meet someone who would change my life forever. That Saturday night finally came and thoughts kept running through my head. I kept thinking, "Don't go. You will save yourself a lot of heart ache if you don't go." But I went.

That night we had one of the biggest storms of the year. It was raining and there was flooding everywhere. That should have been a sign to turn the car around, but I didn't. I took a chance and I am glad I did. We would only be together for a short while, but in that time I had the best relationship one could ever wish for. It seemed too good to be true.

Sadly the relationship had to end as he had responsibilities to his Mom down east. I told him to come back and get me when the kids were old enough to take care of themselves, or when the time was right.

"Another life-time," he used to say. "In another life time

everything will be perfect."

I believe we all are reincarnated in some way. Life just keeps giving us that chance to get it right. It just makes me wonder - how long have we been chasing each other. How many centuries have passed?

People have told me that I am crazy to wait. But I don't think I have a choice. Nobody in my life has ever made me feel the way he makes me feel. It is different from what I have felt before, even with my ex-husband. I've never felt like this, like I've known him all my life.

Do you believe in love a first sight? Do you believe in soul mates? I didn't before - but I do now.

"The best love is the kind that awakens the soul and makes us reach for more, plants a fire in our hearts, and brings peace to our mind."

(From, *The Notebook,* by Nicholas Sparks)

I have found the other half of me...now I am lost.

Jill, 35

John....

Nathan came along when I was 16, and on the rebound from what I later learned was indeed my first love. Dark hair, dark eyes, and skin the colour of an early summer tan – I had heard the rumours about him, but I didn't care. He was the 'bad boy' and every girl had a secret crush on him. He called me on the phone and we would talk for hours. Those calls became more frequent and soon we were talking in the halls at school. I was hesitant to get involved. After all, what would this Grade 11 hottie want with Grade 10 me? But after asking my best girl friend a million times what she thought, I made up my mind and decided to give this guy a shot. He seemed interested and hey, it would probably only be a two week fling so what did I have to lose?

That fling turned into a relationship, and I experienced more than I ever thought I would be capable of. In the three-and-a-half years we were together, I laughed, cried, and had a lot of firsts. Looking back now, I still have fond memories. Near the end of our relationship, I cried more than I laughed, but he was my best friend and I couldn't let go. It was obvious, to me at least, that we had grown apart. I wanted to go to university, meet new people, and figure out who I was. He wanted to work, live at home, and do the same things he had always done.

During the last year of my relationship with Nathan, I met John. John and I worked together at MacDonald's. We talked at work, and then started hanging out together outside of the fast food world. We would drive around in his Jeep, pumping the music, and visiting his friends (who had inadvertently become my friends as well). But, most of all, we talked. Even though John had developed a crush on me (a fact I didn't learn until much later) he listened to my boy problems and gave me advice. But most of all, he gave me a hug when I needed it and tried to keep a smile on my face.

When Nathan and I finally broke up, John and I became attached at the hip. But school was coming, and we both knew that being in different cities wasn't going to work for us.

By the end of my first year of university, I realized that I had let something very special slip away. Not the three-and-a-half year, on-again-off-again, high school relationship with Nathan, but that other one, the one that always made me smile. After an awkward phone call and a two day visit that turned into a long weekend, John and I realized that the two hour drive that separated us geographically could not extinguish our feelings for each other.

Now, almost five years later, the only thing that has changed between John and I is my hair colour and the physical distance. We live together and are still going strong. Where is Nathan? The last I heard he was still living at home, working, and doing what he has always done. We haven't talked in over a year. It's funny how relationships change. It's funny how I've changed.

April, 24

Jeremy....

Jeremy and I shared a love for the outdoors and especially outdoor adventure. Our first dates were treks along hiking trails, but they soon developed into climbing rock faces that stood over 100 feet high. Conversation along the hiking trails was casual and relaxed, while communication atop the cliffs was intense, from exchanges that could save our lives to expressions of exhilaration.

Months of dating evolved into a relationship, and the inevitable question presented itself: was this to become permanent? I had doubts that I had not yet clearly articulated to myself. They began to accompany me, nagging, along our adventures. One day, during a particularly difficult climb, my emotions came into focus. I was standing on a narrow ledge on the Bon Echo rock face, far above the waters. My back was pressed against the rock, all my attention focused on the rope between us. Jeremy had climbed above and was now beyond hearing range. The only communication we had was through the rope; my hands and fingers attuned to the slightest movement, telling me when to hold it tight, when to feed slack through. Finally the movements told me that he had stopped, and would soon signal for me to begin my portion of the climb.

Relaxing my focus, I looked down over the waters of Lake Mazinaw, pondering the complexities of a relationship in which we communicated vital information through a line of rope, trusting each other with our very lives. And there it became clear to me: the bond we had developed on the rocks hadn't, and wouldn't, transfer into the rest of our relationship. When our feet hit the ground, another essential kind of trust was missing, and I knew it always would be.

That adventure was our last together. Occasionally I'm visited by memories of the adrenalin rush you get from looking down from a dizzying height. Mostly, I'm happy to feel the firm stability of earth beneath my feet.

Cheryl, 46

Jeff....

You know that you are in dating trouble when you are 32-years-old and your date's mother says, "Jeff, if the girls are staying the night, you need to clean up your room."

Heather, 46

Jordan, Jason, and Josh....

My relationship with my brothers is obviously not the same type of relationship profiled in the other 99 stories in this book. But it is one worth mentioning. As I have watched my little brothers grow up, I have appreciated more and more how incredibly different they are. Different things touch them and affect them. Jordan is closest to me in age, Jason is the middle brother, and Josh is the baby of the family.

Jordan is one of the most amazing people I know. He and I have been through so much together. He defies the rule that every man has a 'jerk' side. He is calm, sweet, and incredibly thoughtful. He would stand up for the moral right if it killed him. He is so dedicated to his family and friends that nothing could ever come between him and them. He is smart, he is motivated, and I know he will go on to graduate and be successful both in life and love.

Jason is an athlete. He dedicates hours and hours to playing any sport he can fit into his life. Hockey is his main focus, but you can find him playing volleyball, basketball, squash, tennis and baseball. He is incredibly smart, charismatic, and witty. Where his athletic ability and smarts won't get him, his charm will.

Josh is the youngest, but by no means is he left behind. He started drawing before he could walk, and at the age of 12 he has completed entire drawings, to scale, of cities, landscapes, Olympic grounds and just about every imaginable structure. Beyond being talented artistically, he is always ready to hug you or tell you that he loves you. He has a great group of very loyal friends who think the world of him. They would do anything for him – a rare trait in 12-year-old boys.

My brothers represent three different stereotypes of men - the intellect, the athlete, and the artist. I realize that sometimes, as women, we are too quick to judge men. We think the intellectual man has the potential to be boring and too introverted. But Jordan is anything but that. He is extremely funny and he can be called on to be the life of any party.

Some women think that athletes are disrespectful and cocky. However, while Jason is confident, he is a far cry from the 'hockey player' we envision. If you could see him taking care of Josh, or helping my mom with my grandma's wheelchair, or hanging out with our family on vacations, you would see a genuine boy who will eventually treat the woman he marries with the utmost respect.

And, last but not least, some women think the artist is flaky and unreliable. But Josh is one of the smartest kids I know. If anyone in our family needs to remember anything – we tell Josh about it. If we need to know a random fact about something, we ask Josh because he will know. He has every single drawing he has ever done organized in folders. He can even remember everything he has ever drawn, and talk to you about it in detail.

By watching my brothers day-to-day, and for years on end, I see a side of them that not everyone else does. The assumptions about their stereotypes are so inaccurate that it makes me wonder how many guys we write off before we get to know what they are like.
Someday, each of my brothers will make a woman very happy, and very lucky. I think there are a lot of Jordan's, Jason's and Josh's out there. So if you have found yours – congratulations! If you haven't, keep looking. Or wait around a couple of years for my brothers to get a little older ☺

Carissa, 23

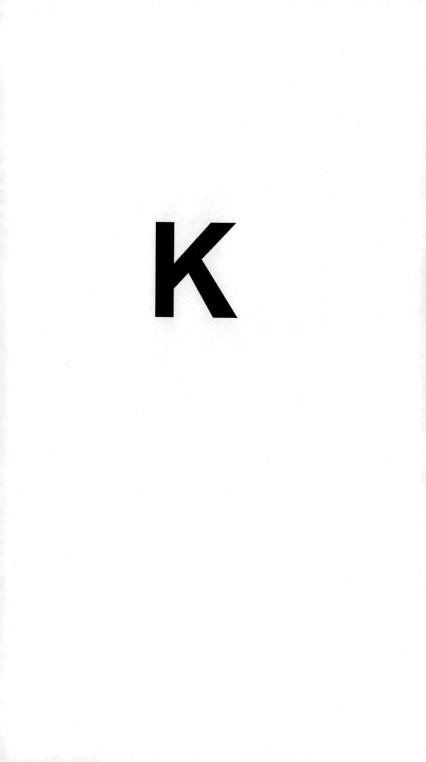

K

Kirk....

It was dark when we left the restaurant and began walking the few blocks home to our apartment. My husband Kirk and I enjoyed walking at night in Japan. The humidity and temperature were finally tolerable, the sound of the cicadas calming, and the darkness created a fleeting veil of anonymity in the small city in which we lived.

As we walked, a faint sound emerged through the quiet night air. It grew louder but in the darkness we couldn't see what it was or where it was coming from. We almost stepped on her before we saw her. Lying on the ground, whimpering with her head on the pavement, her leg bent crookedly under her body, was a small dog that had been hit by a vehicle. The perpetrator was nowhere to be seen. Nearby was a gas station with two young male attendants laughing and talking loudly in Japanese. Kirk and I walked over to them and tried to explain to them with our broken Japanese that the dog had been hit by a car and needed help right away.

The two boys shrugged. Yes, they had seen the dog. But, they said, "Shikataganai," a Japanese expression meaning "Nothing can be done" or "It can't be helped." They explained that if they called a veterinarian this late at night, they would have to pay the fees and they didn't want to do that. The boys turned away and resumed their conversation.

The dog's whimpering turned into a moan and her frightened eyes pleaded to us. An older woman walked by. We tried to ask her for help but her indifference was the same, "Shikataganai." Kirk and I waited but no one else walked by. With our limited Japanese skills, and without any idea of where the nearest veterinarian's office might be, how to contact them, or how to get the dog there, I also began feeling there was nothing that could be done. But I could see Kirk was upset.

"We have to do something," he insisted.

"But what?" I countered feeling helpless.

Kirk phoned one of his co-workers at his school who spoke a bit of English and explained what had happened. The teacher's response was one of confusion. "You got hit by a car?" No, a dog. "A dog got hit by a car?" Yes. "Not you?" No. "A dog?" Yes. "Well...there's not much you can do," he said.

Ahead of us, we noticed a light coming from a small hole-in-the-wall building that we hadn't seen before. A small man sat drowsily behind the desk wearing a local police uniform. Kirk walked into the police office and tried explaining to the officer what had happened: accident... car... dog... hurt...

The officer's ears perked up when he heard the word "accident." He began writing a report. Then he stopped. "Man or woman?" he asked in Japanese. No, a dog. "Man?" No, dog. He wrote some more, looked at us strangely, and kept writing. His face crinkled with confusion. Finally, he nodded his head and indicated that he would send someone out.

We headed home but had trouble sleeping that night, not knowing if the police officer would actually send someone to help the dog, or if she was still there, in the dark, in pain and alone. The next morning before work we drove by the place where we had found the dog the previous evening, but she was gone.

When Kirk arrived at work, his co-worker asked him again: "It was a dog that got hit by the car?" Yes. "Not you or Jacquie?" No. "Well, Kirk, you were very kind to try to help that dog while other people walked by."

Immanuel Kant, the German philosopher, once wrote, "We can judge the heart of a man by his treatment of animals." Those words rang true for me on a quiet evening, late at night, as my husband tried to help an injured dog in a foreign country.

Jacquie, 28

Kal....

My third and final date with Kal was what my dad calls a "crash and burn" date. Kal crashed, and Kal burned. Figuratively speaking, I mean.

The first two dates Kal was a gentleman; sweet, charming, and the brand new BMW didn't hurt his stocks either.

He picks me up and we go for dinner. On the way we're talking about the geography of Southern Alberta, (I don't know why) and he explains that the reason his knowledge is so limited is because he's bad at biology. That's right, biology. Clue number one – this boy is dumb! So we get to the restaurant and we sit beside this loud furnace. So annoying.

Luckily, I'm distracted from the furnace because Kal blows his nose into his napkin. At the table! Clue number two – this boy has terrible manners. I point this out to him and he is actually confused. He needs me to explain that he should go to the bathroom to blow his nose. Gross.

Anyway, we continue talking and the meal is great. But he says the weirdest things. He tells me that now that he has reached the ripe age of 25 he is more mature with respect to dating. Turns out, he used to date good-looking girls. So I try to embarrass him by implying he doesn't date attractive girls anymore and remind him that he is calling me unattractive, which he agrees with! I can't tell anymore if he is blatantly rude or just dumb! We continue conversing and he starts making some weird sucking noise from his mouth. It gets so bad that I actually interrupt myself speaking and forget what I was talking about. I tell him that it is bad manners to make such sucking noises at the dinner table. He says he doesn't know how else to get food out of his teeth. Again, I tell him to go to the bathroom.

This guy annoyed me so terribly I was ready to walk home in the cold wind but then I reminded myself that his BMW had heated seats. So I stayed, but only for a few more minutes.

He drops me off at home. I decide that he will never, EVER, be hearing from me again. I look at him. He has this gigantic cold sore on his lip, at least one square centimeter. I say, "Goodbye" and he replies, "Well, I don't expect you to suck my face tonight..."

Lerina, 24

Kim….

At 21, I could describe to my friends my perfect man: Blond and blue-eyed, an outgoing surfer-type who parties all the time. Since then, every guy I've dated that remotely fits that description turned out to be bad news. Ladies, you know the type. The guy you're attracted to instantly but once you date him you realize he's a cheater, a liar, or worse. Lucky for me, I always had the self-confidence to say, "See ya later" when dating one of those men, even though secretly I wished

I could have turned a blind eye to his faults because he looked so damn hot.

Now I'm 36, and when I think about my husband Kim, who is not a "blond, blue-eyed, outgoing surfer-type that parties all the time" (although he's been known to become "rye-guy" on occasion), I thank my lucky stars I didn't end up with what I thought was my perfect man. Kim did all he could to convince me that he was 'The One' for me. The night I met him I was pining away for an Aussie man I had met while on a bus tour in the United States. This Aussie was my perfect man, or so I thought. He even lived on a beach and was a great surfer. And Kim, well, he just tried too hard and the only thing he convinced me of was that he was annoying. In fact, I tried to set him up with my friend just to get rid of him.

But something has to be said for his persistence. I started dating Kim even though he knew I was planning a trip to Australia. I was going to determine whether or not I truly loved this Aussie and could make a go of it with him in Australia. While I was there, Kim wrote me letters and told me how much he loved me. The Aussie wanted me to stay, but I realized yet again that my 'perfect man' was not who I truly wanted him to be. When I returned, slightly heartbroken, I made it difficult for Kim and didn't want to be in a relationship. And can you believe it? He simply said he would be there for me when I needed him.

And somehow, he knew I would need him.

Kim is my perfect man. We have two perfectly bright and beautiful little girls. My life is perfect. And the moral of this story? Keep an open mind. You can find perfection where you'd least expect to.

Sandy, 36

Ken....

My husband of six years has been so supportive. I have struggled with low self-esteem, depression, and anxiety for most of my life. He has always accepted me as I am but also encouraged me to grow. He saw something in me that I didn't. He encouraged me to be myself and to believe in myself. He helped me see that I had a choice about my attitudes and thoughts, and showed me I could choose to rise above my self-pity.

It has not been easy changing my negative thought patterns, but now I have a healthy view of others and myself. Ken has given me the courage to grow and overcome struggles in my life. I thank God for blessing me with such a wonderful husband and friend. I know that I would not be the woman I am today if he was not a part of my life.

Kristie, 27

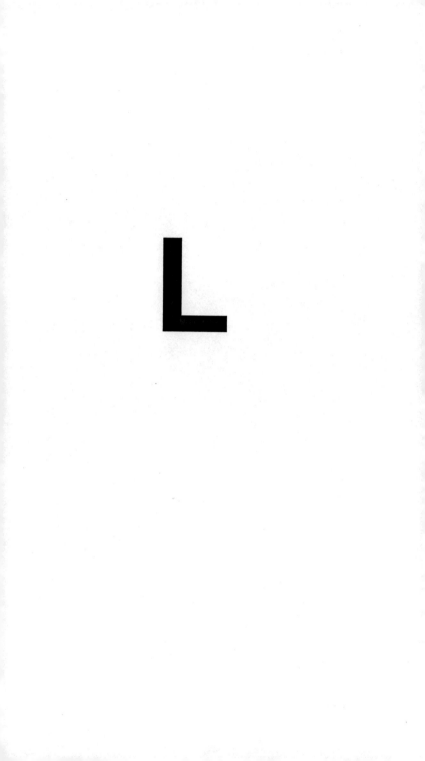

Liam....

Liam and I met when I was in grade nine. I had been home-schooled from grades one to nine and was searching for the high school that I wanted to go to by shadowing grade ten students at various high schools around the city.

I showed up for my shadow day at what ended up being the high school I chose to go to. As soon as I walked into the meeting room I noticed Liam. A grade ten student at the time, he was cute, had a ton of energy and I was instantly drawn to him. He picked up his grade nine student who he was taking on for the day and I found my grade ten mentor. I was extremely pleased to see Liam and his grade nine shadow in my first class of the day!

Through the entire class we kept catching each other's eye and I was totally drawn to this boy that I hadn't even talked to. At the lunch hour, my mentor and I were in the office trying to figure out if there was a drama class that afternoon that I could check out. Out of one of the back rooms popped Liam saying that he had drama in the last block and would be happy to take me to the class. Liam and I ended up hanging out that afternoon and then I didn't see him again until the first day of my grade ten year.

I waited for school to start anxiously so that I could see him again – thinking he wouldn't even remember my name. During registration he came up to me and not only remembered my name, but we ended up chatting off and on throughout the first couple of weeks of school. I ended up running for Student Council and winning the seat of grade ten rep. Liam was one of the grade eleven reps and we spent a lot of time together working on school projects. Our relationship prog-ressed and we ended up dating for the last half of my grade ten year. Although our romantic relationship didn't last forever our friendship has. Liam is still one of my favorite people in the world – someone who can make me laugh harder than almost anyone, and someone who I always look forward to seeing. Ours is a great story to have as my first 'real boyfriend' story.

Rachel, 39

Lauren....

I met Lauren on a fake date.

It was the end of September 1995 and Lauren was the best friend of my boyfriend, Jason.

Lauren was working in the music industry for a small recording studio and publishing company in South-western Ontario. He was going to scout some talent at a downtown London restaurant. It was informal and all, but he and Jason had been talking and they decided that Lauren needed to make a really good impression by having a "hot broad" on his arm to "seal the deal." (Jason's terms of reference and you've got to love the political correctness). Poor Lauren was mortified by Jason's way of getting to the point, but that was Jason.

In any event the two of them came to me and said, "Hey, Brenda, we need you to be Laurens' date for the night. Can you get all dolled up and pretend you are his girl so the prospect will be at ease and Lauren won't be so uptight at the meeting?" I recall thinking that Jason was looking forward to a Saturday night of watching TV in his boxer shorts and consuming as much beer as humanly possible while his girlfriend was out for the evening.

To me it sounded like a chance to have a good laugh

128

at both of these crazy guys. It was also a free dinner and a chance to use my new red lipstick and wear my new red sweater, so I said OK. It was the best offer I had received in quite some time and a girl needs to have some fun.

As dinner progressed I soon realized that the laugh was on me because Lauren was so much more than Jason's goofy pal. The two of them were Mutt and Jeff. Complete opposites. Jason was tall and in wonderful shape for a barrel whereas Lauren was the tallest, skinniest giraffe I had ever shared a meal with.

Yet his green eyes were full of passion for his business and for life. He just had this personality that made me think it was possible to fall in love inside of half-an-hour, over a plate of greasy chicken fingers.

Jason saw a change in both of us when we returned home even though neither one of us had cheated. Jason said, "Y'know, maybe you two belong together and I might be the worlds biggest idiot for helping set this up."

It took a few months for everything to sort itself out. I won't lie and say it was easy. There were arguments and there were times of second-guessing. But true love just gives you the motivation to make it work somehow. Now we all see that I met Jason so that I could meet Lauren. About a year after Lauren and I were married Jason found his soul mate and Lauren was the best man at his wedding.

Lauren and I just celebrated our seventh wedding anniversary and this September 30 will mark ten years since that dinner.

Time has witnessed a lot of changes for Lauren and I, but he still works in music (albeit in Toronto now). We have a long distance marriage as our home is in

London, Ontario. We are committed to one another and his eyes are as green and as passionate as ever. We may be apart Monday to Thursday but our weekends are very special.

I still have that red lipstick but alas the sweater died many years ago in a laundry accident.

I bet the chicken fingers are still as greasy though.

Brenda, 35

Leif....

L is for Leif (he is me life):

Just after university my high school friend, Kristy, and I planned a trip to Honolulu, Hawaii, and Sydney, Australia. In Australia we were going to stay with my sister for three weeks.

In Honolulu, Kristy and I did the tourist attractions including Pearl Harbour. While we were in line a guy from Los Angeles started speaking with us and later on we headed out for drinks.

While we were out we got onto the topic of relationships and I told him that all I ever wanted was to be with a man who I could give into completely. I explained that trust, love and honesty were things I had been seeking since I could remember. In a moment of strange silence he looked me straight in the eye and told me that I would find this man in Australia. We stared at each other for a few moments and then that moment was gone. He gave me his card and insisted that I contact him when I found the man I was looking for in Australia.

When we got back to the hotel, I threw his card away.

That was September 5, 2001.

After arriving in Australia I didn't think twice about the guy in Honolulu. I found myself having the party of a lifetime. We traveled, went out, and met interesting people. I had missed my sister, Laura, a lot and was so thankful to her for letting us stay in her funky flat in the heart of Sydney.

One party night on the town, Laura and I celebrated with a cocktail at a local club. While waiting for our order I sensed the person behind me getting restless and could see out of the corner of my eye that he was pacing sideways trying to get to the bar. After getting our drinks Laura and I didn't move away to let him through. Instead we cheered each other and sipped our cocktails. This annoyed the gentleman behind us immensely. I heard him say, "C'mon Dah'ls get out of the way would ya?"

As a polite girl from Toronto, I turned on my heel with my finger pointed high to instinctively say, "Excuse me buddy...." But as I looked up, up, up, (he is very tall) I looked into the eyes of the man I have been dreaming about my entire life.

"Oh, hello," I said.

Instead of pushing past us to the bar he said, "Oh, I didn't mean you."

Leif introduced himself and so did I. He was immediately intrigued by my accent and I kept looking at how gorgeous this man was and kept talking! He bought us a drink and after exchanging a few more words he excused himself saying, "Well, ladies, have a great time in Sydney!" and walked away.

I was not letting him go that easily. I had met the guy I had been dreaming of since I first watched *The*

131

Silver Lining

Princess Bride! I grabbed Laura and went to find my friend Kristy to show her this amazing man. We shuffled through the crowd, went up and down the stairs from level to level. Finally he was going up the stairs and I was going down and we met again. We grabbed each other's hands. From that moment we never let go.

That was September 7, 2001.

The morning of September 8, Leif pulled up to my sisters' place in a hot car, picked me up, and took me to Bondi Beach for breakfast. We got along unbelievably well.

On the night of September 10, a group of us went out for a farewell dinner. Leif and I were so much in love that night but we had not dared tell each other as Kristy and I were scheduled to fly out on September 11. It was a fate, although sad for many, which kept Leif and I together to this day.

After dinner in beautiful Darling Harbour looking at the Opera House, Leif took us all back to my sisters' place. Leif and I sat outside on the porch front sofa and just held each other. We still hadn't told each other what the other was feeling. For me the fear of rejection was too great. In the past I had said those three words prematurely. I was not going to do this to a guy I had only met four days ago.

Leif and I went into the house so he could say goodbye to the rest of the girls. Laura was on the phone and I could tell that she was speaking to one of my parents. She looked at me with huge eyes and covered her mouth. Since she didn't have a television we couldn't have known what had happened.

That was September 11, 2001.

My parents told Kristy and I that we weren't going anywhere. As we were flying on my dad's airline passes (he works for Air Canada) we were on standby and since all the airports were closed, Toronto included, the snowball effect would see us stranded in Sydney for three weeks.

Leif and I spent this time together with mixed emotions. Sad with what had happened to the world, but overjoyed because we were so in love!

Three weeks later it was time to go. Leif drove me to Sydney airport and we held each other's hand the whole way. This was hard! At the airport Leif told me something that I still get butterflies about when I think of it. It was the first time we had acknowledged that we loved each other.

"Shannon," he said. "I can't believe that in such a short time I could feel this way. I love you. You do know that don't you." I nodded and nuzzled under his neck and in his chest. We cried a little.

"I'm coming back," I said.

He said he knew.

On the plane I wished I had that guy's card. The one from Honolulu who told me this would happen to me.

Three months later I waited at Toronto airport. I was waiting for Leif to come through the frosty doors. That was January 2, 2002. Leif stayed in Toronto with my family for three weeks and I went back with him to Australia.

On December 11, 2004 Leif and I were married. We have lived happily ever after ever since.

Shannon, 28

Mike....

Mike and I met one summer over email. He was the President of the Ski Club at the University of Alberta and I was the Director of Student Group Services. In order for his club to be able to run the following year, I required paperwork from him. Unfortunately, he was working out of town and an online argument turned into a bit of a power struggle. Finally, about six weeks later we had arranged a meeting that worked for both of us.

Going from dreading meeting one another, to flirting our way through the entire meeting, Mike asked me out for lunch "on behalf of the ski club." I responded, "no" once (trying to be tough), but when he asked me again I said, "sure." After all, I had to be on good terms with my student groups...

Our lunch date turned into a three-hour break in the day. We continued to see each other throughout the summer on Fridays for lunch, when Mike was in town. In the fall we started seeing more of each other – but never once did we admit that we liked each other. We definitely never used the term 'dating.' He thought that I wasn't that into him because he felt like I wasn't putting any effort into the relationship. I wasn't putting much effort into the relationship because I thought he wasn't actually into me, and that he was just playing with me. By about December of that year things had faded off. Apparently, you can't sustain a relationship when you can't even admit that you like each other – who knew?

At the time, I couldn't admit to myself that Mike had affected me in a way that no one else had. But I got nervous when I saw his number on my call display, or when I was walking somewhere that I thought he might be. I would sit in front of my computer waiting for a new email to come from him. And I always looked forward to being with him. Yet, I could never bring myself to tell him any of that.

Mike was 'that' guy – the popular one that girls fell for and he was used to always having the upper hand with them. I was so scared of being just another girl to him that I didn't let myself see past his reputation and acknowledge who he really was – a sweet, caring man.

Two years later I had moved across the country, developed a whole new life for myself, and not seen or talked to Mike. Then one day, totally out of the blue, I got an email from him. He was just writing to say "Hi," but we started talking more often and old feelings started resurfacing. Six months later he was on a plane to come and see me.

Mike and I had discussed the visit before he got there, and we purposely decided that it was going to be a visit to catch-up. We decided that nothing could happen between us. Long distance was impossible. However, as soon as we saw each other we knew that would be easier said than done. In the two years that had passed we had grown up, changed, and developed in ways that complimented each other. With a 'no games' rule in place, we had to honestly realize that the feelings we had for each other weren't worth ignoring a second time. So, after trying once and failing due mostly to forfeiting, we were trying again - this time with a country between us, but with a lot more honesty.

Our time together since then has been amazing. We have grown closer, learned more about each other, and our feelings have only gotten stronger. That didn't happen overnight though. I had been single for over three years. I own a company. I moved across the country by myself, and I am the kind of person that does everything by myself – all the time. Stepping into a relationship wasn't easy for me. I had a hard time trusting that I was any different from any of the other girls he had dated. I was so sure Mike was going to let me down. Not because of anything he had done, but because I had convinced myself of that fact three years ago.

I had myself waiting for things to fall apart, instead of letting myself be excited for what the future could hold. It was a weird mix of emotions. I felt so strongly for Mike so quickly, yet I also felt constrained because I knew how much it would hurt if it didn't work out. Luckily, Mike stuck it out. I remember telling him, the very first time he came to Toronto, that being together and making this work was going to be hard for me. He told me he would prove to me that he wouldn't let me down or hurt me – and he has stood by that promise.

Mike has treated me like every girl only dreams of being treated – I could use the whole book to tell the stories. He tells me every day that he feels lucky to be with me and he is excited for our future together. He is also a romantic, leaving me cards with chocolates or gift certificates for my favorite places. Then he goes even bigger.

On my birthday this year I happened to be back home in Edmonton and had a party at a comedy club. Mike couldn't be there because he was the best man in a wedding the next day and the groomsmen were staying together that night. It was a totally legitimate reason, and although I missed him, I understood. About 20 minutes into the show the MC called out my name and asked me to come on stage. He asked me if I knew a "Mike Grand." I said, "Yes. He's my boyfriend." Out from backstage came a huge bouquet of flowers, a gift, and a card that was titled "To the most amazing woman I know." Mike had gone through all the trouble of having the entire surprise organized for me because he couldn't be there himself!

I didn't think that could be topped – until he outdid himself. On the September long weekend my friend and I hosted a little get-together at my condo. At about

Silver Lining

10:30 p.m. someone knocked on my door, I opened it, and there was a big bunny holding a box of chocolates and big yellow cards – instructing me to read them out loud. With everyone in my condo watching, I read the bunny's message telling me that Mike couldn't come to visit me the next weekend (which was what we had been planning for over a month) and he didn't want me to be mad so he had sent me gifts. The bunny handed me a box of chocolates. The last card told me that the biggest present for me was inside the bunny suit and instructed me to pull the head off the costume. Mike was inside! For the last month he had been scheming with my friend to come a week early and surprise me!

Beyond all of the big actions, what means the most to me is how invested he is in our relationship. We have a book club where we read different books that we think will help us improve our relationship. He is committed to getting close to my friends and family because he knows how important they are to me, and he enjoys being a part of my career and is constantly helping me with all the projects I start. Just recently he made the decision to move to Toronto so that he can try something new and so that we can be together.

The decisions he has made to demonstrate his feelings for me have slowly broken down the defenses that I had built up. He has been patient, unbelievably supportive, and extremely caring. He has only been back in my life for a short time, but already I can't imagine my life without him. Mike has brought balance to my life and a new appreciation for just being – not always doing. He has become a constant source of strength, peace, and support. He takes care of me in a way that I never realized I needed. Now, for the first time in my life, I feel comfortable saying that I need someone. I have finally let myself be excited for what the future holds, and it gets more and more exciting every day.

Carissa, 23

Marshall....

This is a story from my mother, who overheard the following conversation...

When I was 6 years old, I was friends with a boy named Marshall. We were neighbours. One day, while playing together in the sandbox, Marshall decided that we should have our first kiss.

He said to me, "Let's kiss."

I replied, "Marshall, I am only 6. I don't think that it is appropriate for me to be kissing boys."

Karen, 28

Martin....

You never know where you'll meet 'The One'.

I was 34-years-old and single. Two male friends, who told me that I'd hadn't been out much lately, bluntly told me I should "not be a such a loser" and should come to this party they were going to.

I tried every excuse to get out of going. It was a cold dark night. I'd rather watch *Law and Order* re-runs in my comfy pj's. "I won't have a ride home because you two will be hitting on girls until 4:00 a.m. and I'll want to go home early," and so on.

On March 15, 1997 I went to this party, begrudgingly and met my future husband.

With that being said...

Silver Lining

Don't be too to quick to judge a guy.

My first date with my future husband, Martin, was a disaster. He invited me to dinner at his place. On the drive to his place, he told that his housemate, Tommy, and his son would be at the house and that I'd only meet them briefly as they were heading out to dinner very soon.

Not quite.

We got to the house. Introductions to were made all around. We made idle chit chat while Martin made dinner. Tommy didn't seem to be in a rush to leave. Next thing we know, Tommy invited himself and his son to dinner. Dinner for two was now dinner for four. Tommy proceeded to get very drunk. He monopolized the conversation. Basically, he hijacked the evening.

One of Tommy's most memorable antics of the evening was when he mentioned, in front of his son, that I'd be spending the night with a drunken nudge, nudge, wink, wink. Martin nearly fell of his chair. I was beet red. The son stared at his dinner plate. At the first opportunity, Martin mentioned that he would be driving me home later that evening.

Thankfully, that drive home came as soon as possible. The front door was barely closed before Martin started to apologize profusely. I could tell he was mortified. He said it was up to me if I wanted to go out again.

When I got home I thought about the evening. What I knew for sure is that I didn't want to go out with Tommy. Martin I was unsure about because I didn't really get a chance to talk to him much.

We had a second date the next weekend, dinner out at a restaurant, just the two of us. Six months later we were married.

Andrea, 42

Mark....

There are a few things that a woman must know about herself before getting into a serious relationship. Lucky for me, I had lots of time to get all of that figured out before any man truly stepped into my life to stay.

Most of my friends will tell you that I am an independent woman. I always have been and I get it honestly from my mother. There is nothing wrong with a woman who knows who she is, what she likes and doesn't like, what she believes in, and how she feels. In fact, every woman should know this about herself before entering into a serious relationship; otherwise it is too easy to take on other people's views and feelings instead of having your own.

I had the fortune of growing up in a rural, small, and beautiful Ontario city surrounded by a group of striking girls, who just so happened to be my closest friends. For years I watched painfully as they all had boyfriends, broke up with them, and then found new love. I was forever the third wheel, and most of the time I didn't really mind. I was, and still am, fiercely independent, confidant, and strong-willed. Something most boys and men didn't find all that attractive because I was intimidating. It didn't help that up until late high school I was taller than most of them – that just added to the intimidation factor.

Along with the many other important decisions that you make in your adolescent years, I made the decision more than once in my young life that I was totally fine being single. Since I was little I knew that I would be just fine if I had my family and good friends. Who needs a boyfriend! Of course there were times I would wonder if I would ever meet Mr. Right, get married, and add to my already wonderful family. As time passed I knew in the back of my mind that when the time was right, I would be ready.

I went to college in Toronto. I didn't know anyone, and once again I made the decision that I was fine being single. I had my own car, job, friends and schoolwork. I decided that I was too busy getting acquainted with my new surroundings. I was waiting for Mr. Right to jump into my life. I didn't have time for Mr. Right Now, nor did I want that kind of relationship. So after finally becoming comfortable with that thought...you guessed it! I met Mr. Right. At the ripe old age of 21 my husband walked into my life.

Now 21 doesn't sound old but on the dating scene, when you have very little experience, it's virtually ancient. I had actually known Mark for a few years because he was a Big Brother to a little guy that I took care of as well, but the timing was never right and we'd never dated.

Neither Mark nor I had much relationship experience except through watching our friends, and the first little bit was interesting as we felt each other out. But as time went on we realized we had a great thing. We didn't know how it was supposed to go, and so we made it up as we went along. We really should have written a script to remember how we did it because it has been better than I could have imagined. We were both individuals going into the relationship with our own lives, friends, family traditions, feelings, thoughts and interests. All of that made it interesting to blend our two lives into one.

We have been together for three years and happily married for about seven months. We are looking forward to growing together through many of the life experiences yet to come. Don't be lead astray - we are human, we are not perfect, and like any married couple we have disagreements and miscommunications. But being your own person going into a relationship helps you become a better person, especially when you are with the right partner.

So for all of those girls like myself who thought they were destined to become an old spinster with a house full of cats, I know that you are going to cringe when I say this...but love finds you when you least expect it!

Heather, 24

Max....

At 16, I fell in love with Max. On our first date we danced in the rain. When he first told me he loved me, he wrote me a song. He said I was pure and sweet. He called me his angelic peach. For every anniversary he gave me a rose for each month we'd been together. My homemade baked bread became an expected staple at all of his family gatherings. For his 19th birthday I made him a quilt for his bed, and for his 20th birthday my family took him on our vacation to Florida – for the second time. On my birthday he bought me a wood and glass display cabinet for the porcelain doll collection I'd inherited from my grandmother. His family frequently talked about us getting married – a real possibility considering three of his older siblings married their high school sweethearts.

At 19, high school graduation meant that everything important to me was ending. A new students council was elected and I stepped out of my position as Prime Minister. After fifteen years of dancing, I performed in my final recital. I danced to a song selected by Max. He watched my solo and then he drove me to school to perform in my twelfth and final drama production. He broke up with me on the way. After the curtain call a friend told me he'd been dating another girl for the last two months. Prom was six days later.

At 24, I spent the Christmas holidays at my parents' home. After a series of random run-ins, I ended up at a party filled with high school classmates on Christmas Eve. As I chatted with a former friend someone entered the room and sat down across from me. I glanced at him, smiled at him, turned to my friend, and then looked back. Max.

He crossed the room, held out his hand and told me to follow him. I followed him as he wandered around the house. He led me to a bedroom, empty except a bare bed. He turned and hugged me. He held me tightly, for a long time. I felt caught. Still he held me longer. Then he sat down on the bed and gestured for me to join him. I perched awkwardly on the edge of the mattress and fiddled with my rings.

He spoke with a tone as though we'd talked only the day before. He said he'd thought about finding me to talk to me. He said I hadn't changed – except my hair was a now little shorter and the colour was not as vibrant. He said some other people had asked about me and how I am. He said I should stop by his new apartment for a visit if I'm ever in Kitchener. He said he'd like me to hear the music he's playing now. He said it seemed like my life was pretty much the same. He said being with me and talking to me felt comfortable.

As he spoke, I studied his face, trying to connect the person in front of me, with the person I spent three years with. His long black hair was shaved bald. His smooth soft cheeks were covered with a full beard and moustache.

He asked me about what I was doing. I talked about finishing school, my new job, the traveling I'd done. I'd forgotten how intensely he looks at me, as though he could see inside me. When we were dating and he looked at me, I connected it with how he felt about me. I loved the way he looked at me then. But now, I felt uncomfortable and somehow uncertain. His eye contact was so direct, clear, held, unchanging. I felt exposed.

He asked me if he'd disturbed me, bringing me upstairs, talking with me now.

"No," I said and searched for words to describe it. "It's surreal." I looked at his penetrating eyes. "I'm sitting here, looking at you and I don't feel like I know you at all. You're somebody I think of and mention in stories and conversations all the time. You were a significant part of my life at a significant time in my life. You hugely affected who I am today. But right now, you sit in front of me and I don't know who you are."

After another half hour of small talk, he asked if I wanted to go downstairs. I followed him and sat in the crowded and smoky living room. He continued to intensely observe me from his armchair across the room.

When I decided to leave, Max walked me to my car. As I fumbled with my purse and empty cookie tray, he stood back, away from the car. He listed his phone number and then cut himself off.

"You'll never remember anyway. If you want to call me, you'll find a way." He stuffed his hands in his pockets. "Merry Christmas. It was really great to see you."

"Thanks." I paused. "You too. Good to see you."

Silver Lining

"Say hi to your family."

"Same to yours."

He turned away and walked towards the house. I started the ignition and headed down the driveway. In the rearview mirror, Max stood in the snow and watched me drive down the river road.

"And that was it," I told my girlfriends three days later over cookies and wine. "The entire time I was around him, I felt like we were on the verge of this big moment - that he was going to say something profound or at least something that would have a profound impact on me, something that would solidify and define this moment. Or I felt like I should be saying something of the sort. But it didn't happen. There was no moment of clarity. It was just this long, drawn-out feeling that something definitive should be happening."

"That was it," my friend explained. "When you told him you don't know him. You loved him, really loved him, but you don't know him."

"Yeah." I sipped my wine. "That was it."

Jeanette, 24

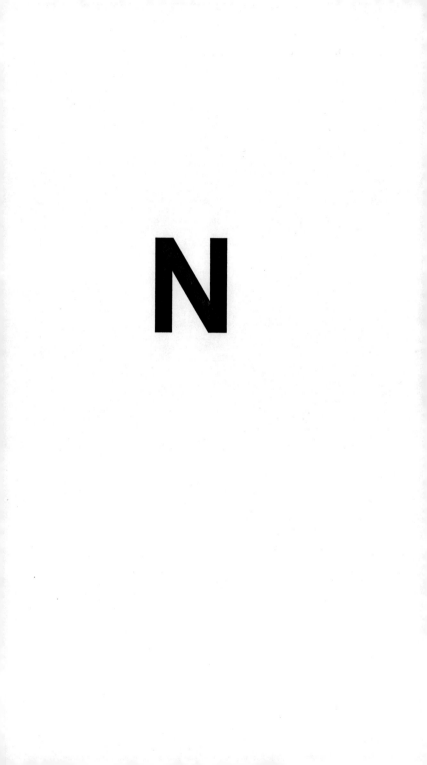

N

Nick....

I asked Nick to join me for pub night at my school. I drove us there since his car was broken. During the drive I mentioned that I had never been to pub night at my school before. Nick suggested that if it wasn't all that great we could go to his school pub, Mugs.

We arrive, order a drink, and I say hello to a few friends. He asks if we're going to Mugs. We'll see, I say. We hang out a little more, mingle a little and he asks again if we're going to Mugs. We've been there barely half-an-hour and he's now asked me 3 times if we're leaving. I can tell he's not having fun, and being the nice person that I am I wasn't going to make him stay there if he wasn't enjoying himself. We leave and make the half-hour drive to his school.

When we get there Nick says, "I may leave you for a minute."

"You can't leave me in a place where I don't know anyone. I've never been here before."

We get inside and he says, "I'll be right back. I just have to say hi to a friend."

He leaves and comes back quickly. Five minutes later he says, "I'll be right back." This time I'm left alone for 15 minutes.

This happens again and again all night long. After two hours I make the excuse that it's time to go because I have an early class. I drop Nick off at home and he is none the wiser that I'm mad at him. The only reason I didn't just leave without saying a word to him was because he was drunk and so were all of his friends. I didn't know if he had enough cash for a cab, and being the nice person that I am, I didn't want to leave him stranded. If I could do that night over I would change a few things.

I would have gone to my car and waited half-an-hour. If he didn't come looking for me I would call his cell and tell him I'm leaving, and if he wants a ride he has one minute to get his ass out here or I'm leaving without him!

Christina, 21

Neil....

Like all women, I have played the dating game. I have met men, fell in love and then had my heart broken into a million pieces. After this happened, I would ask myself, why did this happen? What's wrong with me? Why didn't he love me the way that I loved him?

Then I met Neil. Well, let me redefine that. I have known Neil for years. He was my best friend.

I had just returned from Brazil and was looking for a place to live for the summer. I happened to sublet in a house where Neil was living. My first afternoon there I was sitting outside and he sat down next to me. He started asking me relationship questions as he had fallen in love with a woman who broke his heart into a million pieces. From there, our friendship was born!

We lived together for a year while I was in New Zealand. Neil completed university and decided to backpack Australia for a year. I met up with him in the Land Down Under and had some of the greatest experiences of my life. He became my other half and I fell in love.

It was when we returned to Canada that things started

to go wrong. I was looking for ways to sabotage our relationship. I was so insecure with myself I didn't believe that I deserved to be happy. I thought that I needed to break his heart before he had the opportunity to break mine.

But the good thing about falling in love with my best friend is that he already knew all of my troubles, my fears, my doubts and my skeletons. And he loved me anyway.

Some days I look at my life, and the way I treated Neil and I thank God that he is still in my life. It took a long time for me to realize, but I do deserve him. I deserve to be happy. Whatever happened in the past is gone. I can't change the things that have happened, but I can learn from them and move on to better things.

I hope that every woman finds her soul mate. I have been blessed in finding mine!

Colleen, 26

Nick....

I was busy making other plans when Nick came along.

About five years ago I ended a relationship that left me with a lot of doubts, questions, and an enormously broken heart. It seemed that I was attracted to men who basically had issues. In my mind, "the more tragic the better." I thought I could help them, heal them, and keep them safe. I finally realized that some things are much bigger than me. I couldn't expect to keep giving all of my heart and soul without getting even a little something in return.

Silver Lining

So I tried online dating. After exhausting that for a year-and-a-half, I was ready to pack it in and remove my online profile. I was going to go abroad and teach English. It was the perfect plan. I had nothing holding me down, I loved to travel and I was taking a TESOL course so I could teach anywhere I wanted.

Then I got a virtual smile from Nick. I figured it didn't hurt to smile back. After a few messages we lost touch for a few months, but reconnected online once again. I wasn't really interested but continued the conversation because he seemed nice enough. After two months of emails and MSN, we spoke on the phone and planned our first meeting. I had seen his photo (which did not do him any justice whatsoever!) but I figured it didn't hurt to meet him. Besides, I had made a decision to change my life and go away for a while. I figured he could turn out to be a great friend.

A simple meeting turned into a three hour gab session. We started our relationship, but I was still hesitant. I had a lot to learn about real relationships because I had a hard time communicating my feelings. In my past relationships I would avoid arguing because I thought it would cause a break-up. I've since learned to have a little more backbone! Nick started teaching me how to trust and depend on him, and express my feelings – something that was completely foreign to me. I was the one who could be trusted and depended on, and I found it very hard to let myself trust and depend on someone else. Nick was like no one I had ever known. He was honest, caring, goal-oriented, funny, and romantic. This was a whole new world for me, but one I knew I could get used to.

A month into our new relationship he took me to Niagara Falls. He made me a personalized CD with a poem asking me to be his girlfriend. Then he gave me a bottle of wine with a label that read, "To be opened on the walk." He meant our walk down the aisle.

Anyone else would have run because it was such a bold assumption, but surprisingly I didn't - I felt the same way. I made the decision, just days before, to stay in town in order to give us a chance.

It's now two years later and we are newlyweds.

Through all of this I have learned that chivalry is not dead, that you should never say never, and I'm a firm believer that love happens when you least expect it.

Stephanie, 29

Nate....

I don't have the greatest track record with relationships, especially the early ones. My first two relationships followed hard upon one another.

It was my first year of University and I was involved with my first real boyfriend, if you even want to call him that. His name was Nate. He was in the fourth year of my program, and he would always come over to sit with my friend and I in the lunchroom on our spare periods. Nate was really nice, had interests similar to mine, and was fairly intelligent. We got along well, but I was hesitant at first. I was a late bloomer and had never really dated anyone. On a more superficial note, I'm a tall girl and he wasn't a tall guy. But in the end, I was willing to overlook the Amazon vs. Hobbit issue and just go for it.

We started spending more time with each other at school during that first week. On the Friday night I went to Nate's house to watch a show we both liked. We'd see each other around and our lunchtime conversations continued, but I really wasn't feeling anything more than friendship for him. During this time we never actually went on an official date; we just saw each other around and one night he drove me home.

I was also doing a course on weekends, and it was here that I met a guy I really liked. I didn't do anything with him except have coffee once, but the way I felt around him made me realize that things with Nate weren't going well. So back at school on the Monday, two weeks after we started 'dating' (we'd only seen each other five times), I decided to tell Nate that I didn't think things were working out between us.

I asked him to take a walk with me on a spare period. I told him that while I really liked him, I didn't think that we were meant to date each other and that, in my opinion, it would be better if we just remained friends. He seemed to accept this readily and easily, and we called off our so-called relationship. But two periods later, he found me again. At a table in the cafeteria, he sat across from me and started questioning why I was breaking it off. I reiterated all my reasons, after which he asked, "Why do I feel like you're lying to me?" I really didn't have an answer to that (well…I did…but I didn't think it would help matters much). He was convinced I had ulterior motives for wanting to end things. After about 40 minutes of back and forth, a couple more accusations, and a final sigh, Nate accepted that I wasn't going to change my mind. He left, and that was the end of that. Things were slightly awkward for a while, especially when I later found out that he had originally liked the friend I sat with at lunch but went for me because I "showed interest." Ouch.

Soon after Nate and I split up, I started dating the guy I had met on the weekend course. Things went well for about a month, until I started wondering why I had never met any of his friends, and why he'd drive us to Woodbridge to see movies when we both lived in Brampton. But I was young, stupid, and far too trusting. Needless to say, we continued dating until one night when we were watching a movie in my room and my phone rang. The conversation with the girl on the other end went something like this...

"Hi"

"Uh....Hi."

"Can I help you?"

"Yeah...Um...My name is Tanya.... and you're dating my boyfriend."

It's not the nicest thing to hear when you're cuddled up with a guy you like. So I asked Tanya how she got my number, and it turned out that she had scrolled through his address book while they were on their camping trip together the previous weekend. She found my number and decided to call me. I was fairly upset at this point, so I asked her if she wanted to talk to him. She freaked out because he was there. So I did the only thing I could. I handed him the phone.

Giving him five minutes to talk alone, I later went back and told him to get the hell out of my room. Obviously this relationship was also ending. He called me for about a week after that – crying each time and telling me that nothing was going on with him and Tanya anymore – but I'd had enough.

I guess I should have known this was coming. A big clue should have been the night I was at his house and his parents came home. They all started arguing with one another, and then his mother drove me home. Her parting words were, "He needs some time alone. Our son has issues." Apparently truer words were never spoken.

Marsali, 23

Omar....

Omar had been trying to talk to me all night at the bar. Not only was he trying to chat - he was trying to convince me that he was a heart surgeon. He looked more like a used car salesman than a heart surgeon. I was walking out of the bar at the end of the night and he stopped me and said, "Listen. These are the facts. I'm rich and you are hot. So we should go out." Why in the world do guys think that these lines will work?!

Caleigh, 19

Otto....

My Grandma was 20-years-old when she discovered that she was pregnant with my mother. Her boyfriend at the time abandoned her. He left her alone, pregnant, and in the care of her rather abusive parents. She was only a few months pregnant when an electrician, Otto, came over to fix some of the electrical problems in the house.

Otto was a 27-year-old German immigrant who was attending school to become an engineer. He said he fell in love with my Grandmother the first time that he saw her. After that first meeting he would stop by often to take her out for ice cream, to the movies, or for long walks in nearby parks. She still hadn't told her parents she was pregnant, and she decided it wasn't fair to continue to date Otto without telling him the truth. However, she was scared and she began to avoid him.

At this time, she was a telephone operator in Toronto. Otto showed up every day for a week with flowers. He gave them to her as she was leaving work. She tried to continue to ignore him, but finally she told him the truth. She was crying and frightened. It was the first time she had said the words out loud to anyone but her ex-boyfriend. Her father was an alcoholic, and she was terrified about how he would take this 'blot' to the family name.

Otto proposed to my Grandmother on the spot, and they were married a few weeks later. Shortly after, my mother was born. She was incredibly close to her father, Otto, and she was his pride and joy from the moment she entered his world.

Otto died when my mother was just 23. He had a heart attack in his sleep. My mother learned that he was not her biological father at the reading of his will. In it, he left a message for my mother telling her that he never had another child with my Grandma because he always wanted my mother to know that he loved her like his own child, and that she was the greatest accomplishment in his life. Similarly, he left a message for my grandma telling her that he did not marry her because she was pregnant, but that he was thankful she had been.

My mother never bothered to look for her 'biological' father. She felt she knew the father that she was meant to have, the father she was blessed to have. However, she did choose to adopt her second child because she realized that biology has little to do with being a parent. My Grandma never remarried, and her eyes still feel with pride when she speaks of her husband, Otto.

I never met my Grandpa, but I've been told stories of him doing gymnastics in the backyard. He was supposed to be an Olympic gymnast in Germany, but after the war he fled to Canada. He gave up on his Olympic dreams and replaced them with new ones.

My Grandma doesn't know that I know this story. She is still ashamed that she got pregnant out of wedlock.

She was afraid I would think poorly of her if I ever found out. I wish I could tell her that I know. I want her to know how proud I am of her and my Grandpa. To me, it is stories like theirs that truly represent love. They're not about flowers, love notes, or chocolates; they're about self-sacrifice, understanding, devotion, passion and friendship. And sometimes - maybe a little bit – they're about fate.

Jewels, 23

Oliver...

There is an old saying that says, "You may forget what they said, you may forget how they said it, but you will never forget how it made you feel." This is a story about "how it makes you feel."

I am fortunate enough to have sifted through all the bad men, all the self absorbed ones, and all the ones who simply didn't get me.

Oliver is a truly amazing man, life partner, and friend. I can sum up the wonderful dynamics of our relationship in his marriage proposal to me.

We had been together for three-and-half-years. In August 2005 he proposed. The setting was breathtaking. We were away on a mini-vacation. It was dusk, there was candlelight…it was truly romantic!

The best part of the evening is the part that I remember the least. I have no recollection of what Oliver said to me the moment he got on his knee to propose. Strangely enough, I will never be able to relive it word for word. But it didn't matter, quite the opposite. The feeling that I had at that moment was profound and unforgettable.

Silver Lining

I asked Oliver to tell me again what he had said to me that night.   He told me, and after a couple minutes, when he was finished, I said, "I cherish you too."

Heather, 30

Parker....

I found myself dating two guys at the same time, Parker and Clive. They were both really great guys and I was having trouble picking between the two of them. I had plans to go out bowling with Clive and his friends. That afternoon Parker called to see what I was doing that evening. I had to make up a family obligation to get out of plans with him without looking like I was brushing him off.

I was having a great time with Clive when Parker walked in with all of his buddies. Horrified, I fled to the washroom to call a girlfriend for advice. I was starting to think I would have to stay there for the rest of the evening when I saw the urinals. In my panic I had run into the men's room! That is where Parker discovered I had lied about my evening plans. From there on in I decided to focus on one man at a time.

Susan, 25

Patrick....

Patrick is my "how did I not see what I was doing?!" story. We started dating in high school – he was a year younger than me and we were totally different people. I was on student's council and the honour roll, he skipped school and never did homework. I worked with youth groups on Friday nights and he partied. Despite our differences we somehow dated for three years. We broke up twice – and got back together. I had always preached to my friends that "if you keep on breaking up there is obviously an issue that is not being fixed – and that is a sign the relationship should just be over." I should have taken my own advice.

Silver Lining

Patrick's family was messed up – to say the very least. With over controlling parents who were abusive to him and his sisters, Patrick had scars and skeletons from his past that just kept on surfacing the longer we were together. I thought I could save him – I thought I could figure out how to make it better. I remember thinking to myself that if I just stuck it out – this is what love meant – being there for someone in the good and the bad.

Everyone questioned why I was with Patrick. It didn't make any sense to anyone who knew both of us. I just kept telling everyone that I knew he had potential. I knew that he was capable of great things and I thought if I left him he might not be able to reach them. I was convinced I had to wait it out, help him along the way, and make it work. I remember telling my friends that you can't date potential. Should have taken my own advice on that one too…

After ongoing issues, struggles and lies, my parents offered to pay for him to get counseling. The final straw was his mom – not him – if you can believe it. We were at his house watching TV when all of a sudden his mom came downstairs and started screaming at me, totally out of the blue. She told me she was sick of Patrick and I being together and that he was with me too much. (We purposely spent almost all of our time with his family and hardly any with mine so that he wouldn't get in trouble). She told me I was a slut (I had been dating Patrick for almost three years and I hadn't slept with him). She told me my parents should be ashamed of the way they raised me (I was a straight–A student, ran youth groups, I started a non-profit organization, I didn't drink, swear, or do drugs. I was as straight laced as they come). She told me that she was embarrassed to see her son with me in public and that when I was with him I brought shame to their family name.

It was an absolute nightmare from then on. For three months I tried to make it work and finally one day I woke up and I realized that this is not how I wanted my life to be. I remember thinking that it would be horrible to have to dread every holiday because I would know that I would have to deal with in-laws. I came to the shocking realization that I had not been happy or laughed with Patrick in over six months. I realized I was waiting for something that Patrick had shown no indication would ever come to fruition. He wasn't helping himself and therefore I couldn't be a support for an action that wasn't happening.

After losing thirty pounds and going down to an extremely unhealthy weight of ninety-seven pounds, almost failing my first year of university and putting all aspects of my life on hold for someone who wasn't willing to help himself, I woke up and realized that not only was I not helping Patrick, I was killing myself. We broke up.

I thought my world would come crashing down around me – but instead it was like a thousand pounds had been lifted off my shoulders. Moving forward from that time I have implemented many of the lessons I learned into my life – and I hope that others who watched me go through my relationship with Patrick that have learned them as well. You really can't date potential. If you are unhappy more than you are happy, it is not a healthy relationship. One person can't carry a relationship.

I am now in a healthy relationship. I get support when I need it and I give support when he needs it. He is as invested in the relationship as I am and I am one thousand times happier than I thought I was with Patrick. My advice: If it isn't right but you are scared to let go, just think about how great things are with this guy when things are going well. Then imagine how much better they would be if you were with the right guy – and they were good all the time.

Ashley, 29

Peter....

Back in the days when I was in high school, it was still very important to find a good man, marry, and settle down to raise a family. I came from an abusive home and was scarred emotionally and sexually, although I did a good job of hiding it. I was not officially allowed to date until I was fifteen, but P. and I had been a number since the summer of eighth grade. I was 'his girl' from the ages of 13 to 17, when we broke up. P. was older than I was by a couple of years. We met in a drama class and found that we both loved history and that we had a great deal to talk about. We started seeing a lot of each other, unofficially of course. His friends became my friends. I had no friends because I chose to be a loner. He was the only person in high school that I trusted to get close to me. He was completely non-threatening because all he wanted to do was kiss and hold hands. That was alright by me. I was still fighting off my father's more serious attentions at home.

Things came to crisis point when P. went off to university. Several months later he asked me to marry him. I was stunned. I was 17-years-old and had two more years of high school to complete. Things were terrible at home and I would gladly have fled the situation, but P. was the only boy that I had ever dated and I was no longer sure that we were right for each other. It had been my hope that he would go away to university and date other girls, and that I would have the opportunity to date other boys.

170

My mother suggested that I make a list of the pros and cons of getting married. I shocked the hell out of her (this woman's middle name was Denial) when I said that I was fairly certain that P. would never hit me, and listed that as the first pro. But I was serious! I had learned that much from dear old Dad. I never wanted to marry anyone like him.

In the end, the cons outweighed the pros, and I declined P.'s marriage proposal. To this day, I do not know if it was the right thing to do. The truth was that I was not ready for marriage. I had no idea what a good marriage would even look like. If I had married P. and ignored the list, I would have married him out of desperation in order to escape from a horrible home environment, and that would not have been fair to either of us. But these insights came later, after a good deal of therapy.

I heard through the grapevine years later that P. married a wonderful woman and that they were very happy together. I am glad for him. He was the first decent man I ever knew. I would like to thank him for that wherever he is. He helped me to establish key characteristics that I wanted in a boyfriend. He showed me that not all men were bad, or to be feared.

Anonymous, 52

Quotes....

In the absence of ANY stories about a man who has a name starting with the letter 'Q', we have put together some quotes – advice we hear ourselves giving to others and things people have told us.

Before you get married you have to agree on three things: kids, religion and money.
Sarah's 85-year-old Grandma

You can't date potential.
Carissa

A woman wants a man, not a child. Don't fall into the trap of becoming his mother.
Carissa

Don't marry too young – you need to know yourself before you make that kind of commitment.
Sarah's Mom and Dad

Make sure you marry well so you can pay me back and take care of me when I am old.
Carissa's Dad

If you are upset more than you are happy in a relationship, you shouldn't be there anymore.
Carissa

You can't change people, and some are just shallow.
Sarah's Mom

Dating doesn't have to be about finding a partner.
Carissa

Sometimes it is better to keep your mouth shut.
Sarah

Silver Lining

If he hasn't called you and you are freaking out…
Don't! Just don't pick up the phone. Get busy.
Sarah

When he says he doesn't know how to use the
dishwasher, he is lying.
Carissa and Sarah

If they still live at home, leave.
Carissa

If he spends more time doing his hair than you do, you
are not compatible.
Sarah

I'll never date a guy who has thinner thighs than me.
Carissa

If you're taller than your man in heels, get over it. Love
your heels, love your height, love yourself.
Sarah

Relationships aren't easy. Don't be lazy – make sure
you're both putting in the effort.
Sarah

Test: Cook dinner for him. Does he offer to do the
dishes?
Sarah

First impressions are very important in dating. Before
your judgement gets clouded by the good sex you had,
make sure you know what this guy is all about and
listen to your intuition.
Sarah

Dating Tip: If he shows up with roses on the first date –
ditch him.
Carissa (Sarah disagrees)

Meeting someone on the Internet, dating them and then breaking up before ever meeting them in person doesn't count as a real relationship.
Carissa

I'm not intimidating.   Maybe you just have low self esteem.
Carissa

In all the excitement of a new relationship, don't forget your friends and family.
Sarah

You don't have to have everything in common, you just have to appreciate your differences and learn from each other.
Carissa

If a man still buys comic books, he is a not a man. He is a boy.
Sarah

Put the toilet seat down!
Carissa

Respect yourself enough to let go of people who don't respect themselves.
Sarah and Carissa

You can't fix someone.   They have to want to fix themselves.
Carissa

You can be independent and successful and still want your door opened for you.
Carissa

Silver Lining

If you are not happy, why are you still there? You are worth more than that.
Sarah

The first time he hurts you it is his fault, the second time he hurts you it is your fault.
Carissa

If it seems like him and his ex are too close – they probably are.
Sarah and Carissa

Don't lose yourself in a relationship. He fell in love with you for a reason. You.
Sarah

Its not that I can't cook. I just don't.
Carissa

If you feel that you are trying to express something important and he has a blank look on his face, it probably means he is emotionally challenged.
Sarah

Spend time doing nothing with your partner.
Carissa

Read 'Men are from Mars, Women are from Venus.' Trust me.
Carissa

Everyone has a decision to be happy or right. Choose to be happy.
Carissa's boyfriend

Ryan....

The Kiss ... a warm swirl of vibrant gold, exploding like sweet, sugary snowflakes onto the tip of my tongue…

Ryan and I made out at my cousin Emily's wedding. Over seventy-five guests had been invited, and we were crammed into the front living room of my Aunt's Toronto home, waiting for the bride to make her way down the circular staircase.

"Who's getting married again?" asked Mr. Rittenbok, a neighbour.

"Emily," I whispered into his wrinkled ear. "Your neighbour's daughter. You've lived beside them for 32 years," I explained to the cute, sweet man sitting beside me, holding onto his black, wooden cane in the leather armchair. Five minutes later, the bridal song started.

After the appetizers were nearly finished, and the cutting of the cake, I found myself alone in the kitchen. While I was looking through my Aunt's cluttered cupboards for a clean teacup, I noticed the videographer, one of Emily's brother's friends, coming at me from behind with his camera.

"What are you doing?" I curiously asked. "The party's not in this room."

"I see beauty everywhere," I remember him saying to me, in a deep, throaty voice that sent shivers through my spine.

"Really," I said, sarcastically. "But you've got your camera pegged on my butt," I replied feeling strangely confident with my current flirting ability at the time. I was expecting him to stop filming, put the camera on

181

the table and say, "You're right. You caught me. That's what I was doing and I apologize. I'm sorry; I guess I got carried away." Instead he said, "Mind smiling for the camera now?" And there was something in his smile that made me comply.

Then I poured him a cup of tea and invited him to follow me into the back den, where we enjoyed a few minutes alone together.

"So how old are you?" I finally asked.

"25," he replied. "You?"

"31," I said, smiling. "And what's your name?" I asked, placing my hand down on top of his left thigh.

I know! Totally a cougar move, but I just couldn't help myself … not that he was complaining.

"Ryan," he said, smiling huge. "What's *your* name?"

"Christine," I replied. "Would you like to kiss me Ryan?" And he did, and it was fabulous! It was everything a kiss *should* be. And I wasn't thinking potential boyfriend or casual fling, or anything really … Ryan and I were just kissing.

We continued to kiss for over ten minutes, and then I pulled away from him and we stopped. I thanked Ryan for his kiss. And he thanked me back.   Then we went back out into the wedding party and mingled.

I spent the rest of the evening dancing to Frank Sinatra records with my Grams and her crazy friend Benny from the Senior's Club, and Ryan captured every moment of it on film.

When the party was over and Ryan was packing up his camera equipment to leave, there was no exchange of numbers or inquiries of meeting again at a later date.

I think Ryan was sent into my life for a moment; for a reason, not a season. I'll probably never see him again, nor do I need to. But I will always remember his kiss.

Shoe, 34

Rob....

Persist: *v.i.* continue in a state or action in spite of obstacles or objection.

It was Saturday night and my friend Michelle and I were at a 'hoe-down' event that happens in Toronto every year. I'm originally from Saskatchewan, and I grew up on a farm, so I figured the hoe-down would be a good change of scenery from the city nightlife.

As Michelle and I walked around I noticed a couple guys close to our age, but I didn't initiate eye contact or anything. Well, these guys took things into their own hands and immediately started chatting us up. Rob came straight for me.

The only thing I truly recall Rob saying was, "Whoa! You're smokin'! You and me? We're hangin' out!! You may not know it yet...but we're hanging out." I chuckled and thought, *Yeah right buddy, that's ridiculous*, but he was entertaining and what else was I going to do?

Next thing I remember, he asked me if I liked his pants. His focus went to his red zipper. *Oh my gosh! Now this guy was directing my attention to his 'finer assets'.* I couldn't bring myself to REALLY look at him, and I couldn't believe him. I was laughing. It was shock value after shock value with this guy; the things that kept coming from his mouth were unreal!

"Oh, so you used to play hockey?"

"Yeah, I used to play professional hockey in the junior division and the ECHL. Feel my ass! That's a nice ass huh?"

I'm not feeling your ass buddy. I don't even know you! Jeez, you are really proud of yourself!

Hockey players are so cocky. I grew up around them in Saskatchewan and while I love hockey, I know hockey players. *This guy is really digging a grave for himself.* However, Rob's approach with everything somehow made me laugh. As cocky and as ambitious as he was, it was easy to talk to him.

Then I found out that he played with the Toronto Fire Department Hockey Team. In fact, he's was the captain. Not only THAT, but he attended York University part-time - taking psychology. AND, he was an actor. In fact, he belonged to the Actors Union.

What? So you are a full-time fire fighter, an actor, you manage to go to university, AND you play hockey? Are you Superman? What else do you do? How is it possible to do all these things?

But here was my logic…

Actor, hockey player, and fire fighter – they all require that 'hero-chicks-dig-me' persona. I didn't want anything to do with a relationship, let alone hang out with some cocky 'hero.'

At the end of the night he asked for my number. I told him no! "Well, how are we supposed to hang out?" he asked. I just laughed. This guy was relentless! He had been drinking a bit so I figured I'd test his abilities. If he was really interested in me I figured he could remember my email address.

I considered giving him a fake email address. I've done it before, we all have. A fake phone number, a fake name, and a fake email…But something inside my head spit out the real email address.

The day after the hoedown he tried emailing 30 different spellings of my name @yahoo.ca, .com, hotmail.com, boxnet.ca, sympatico.ca, etc. He tried everything and finally one got through to me. He asked me to go for coffee.

Unfortunately, I was going out of town and I wasn't sure of my schedule. I made sure to take my signature off the bottom of my response so he didn't have my phone number. I couldn't believe this guy actually remembered my email and was contacting me. Ahhhhh!

A week went by and I received another e-mail asking me to go for coffee. Like the last one, I explained that I'd be out of town.

I returned from my travels and realized that I had a phone message from this guy. *How did he get my phone number? He's asking to go for coffee AGAIN. I don't believe this.* I checked my home phone messages, and there was a message from him there too. *How did he get my numbers?* And then I realized that, 'silly me,' I forgot to take my signature off the e-mail before SENDING it to him, and he got my number. If you call my cell it says, "If you can't reach me here, try me at home…" *Great, this guy is now stalking me. I can't believe the effort he's putting into me.*

185

I agreed to go for coffee with him, just to put him at rest. *Besides, it might be nice to see him again.* I needed to tell him why I wasn't interested in him and why I didn't want to get involved. I didn't want to get hurt. I was enjoying being single. I was enjoying not having to fulfill 'girlfriend' duties.

We went for coffee. I was a bit nervous because I hadn't seen him since the hoe-down. Would I recognize him? I remembered him being shorter than me and sort of arrogant. In fact, he was taller than me, and very muscular, being a fire fighter and all. He seemed pretty genuine, and he had a very good sense of humour. I laid everything on the table when we went for coffee, which ended up turning into lunch. Rob was funny! He was honest about his past and present relationships, his feelings...everything! I really enjoyed my time with him.

When he dropped me off, he asked if we could get together again sometime. I thought it might be fun, but I was going out of town again. I said to try me after I got back into town. He emailed me a couple of times while I was out west, and his emails were very entertaining. He asked if I needed a ride from the airport and as cautious as I was, I gave in and accepted his offer. I didn't want him to think that this meant anything, so I kept things very casual and on a 'buddy-buddy' basis. He was a nice guy...

One night, a little while later, he called and left a message on my answering machine asking me to call him back. I didn't feel comfortable calling him back because I didn't want to lead him on. *I could just disregard the message and wait to reply to his next e-mail...*But something inside me felt I owed it to him to dial his number. I finally called him when I got home and we chatted on the phone for a good hour.

He asked if I wanted to go to St. Lawrence Market the following weekend. I thought it would be nice, fun, and casual. *He knows I'm not interested in getting involved.*

I woke up that Saturday and I wasn't feeling very good. I wasn't enthusiastic about seeing Rob and hanging out with him either. The situation felt too much like a date. It made me nervous.

He called and I told him I wasn't feeling very well and I'd have to cancel on him. He was already on his way to pick me up. I felt terrible. He wanted to drop something off for me since he was already on the way. I quickly dolled myself up. When I heard the knock on my door I took a deep breath. Behind that door was Rob - the most nervous, yet confident guy you've ever met. He was holding a bouquet of white roses with two red roses sticking out (he said I had to earn the rest), a bottle of red wine, and a card. Standing in the hallway of my apartment with the door wide open, he couldn't stop talking and babbling nervously.

I was laughing and gushing at how cute he was. I told him to shut up and invited him into my apartment. I told him to chill out. It was just me he was talking to. That's the one thing with Rob – other guys might make me feel nervous or insecure, but from the very beginning I've always felt really comfortable in front of him.

Rob sat down and told me that as confident as he is, I made him second-guess every word in every email we'd ever exchanged. He told me that I made him want to be a better man, and that he really wanted the opportunity to get to know me better. He kept repeating himself. I reminded him to breathe and relax. It's just me. I opened the card, and he offered to make me dinner as we shared the bottle of wine he brought. It turned out we were sharing a bottle of red wine from 1975 that was given to him from his Italian relatives. He was told to share it with someone special.

It's funny because he'll say to this day, "You gave me nothing!" It wasn't until December, at his favorite restaurant, when his 10-year-old niece asked, "Faye, are you my Zio's girlfriend?" our relationship became official. Rob and I just looked at each other and started laughing. I'm grateful she asked us to confirm things. I committed myself to Rob as my boyfriend in front of his three beautiful nieces. I was a girlfriend. Was I ready for it? *Yep, I like this guy. If I enjoy being with him, if it's easy to be with him, if I can laugh and have fun with him, then…yep! I must like this guy. I'm ready to be a girlfriend.*

Rob is confident, honest, sweet, original, genuine, and sincere. We have been together for a year and I love him more and more as each day passes.

Faye, 30

Rick….

I'm standing on the steps of the church. The sun is shining; the day is perfect in every way. My father looks sternly at his watch. I scan the street for a green Plymouth, pushing the veil back from my 'face and feeling my hand slick with sweat on the handle of my bouquet. If he were there, now in the street, I would bolt and never look back. But he isn't there and I turn to a choice made from fear and the expectations of others.

In the moment my emotions get sealed over, but my heart will break in a hundred tiny shards over the years. Every time my heart breaks, I think of him.

I imagine his life as perfect. I try to fake some kind of twisted nobility convincing myself that I made the best choice for him. By leaving him, by not begging to see him when he called three months before the wedding to see if I was really serious. I sensed unnamed demons lurking. Terrors, misery and ugliness seeping around the edges but still beautifully lacquered over unrecognized. But somewhere in that reptilian, survival brain, I must have known he could never cope and would shrink away in distaste and fear. I couldn't risk the picture I knew he held of me. Still pure, still whole, still separate from what was waiting for me. That thing that would set me apart forever from others. Unclean, unlovable, unworthy.

Heather, 46

Ryan....

Remember ladies, "Where were you? I was worried" is protective.

"Where the **** were you? Who were you with? I want to know where you are!" is possessive. Possessive is generally not good.

Johanna, 24

Richard....

When I was ten, a child by most definitions, I had an active imagination. I had a husband named Seth. We sailed around the world together. Later, I divorced him. Then I married Logan. We had children together. Our oldest daughter was named Adele. She was my

Silver Lining

Cabbage Patch Doll. With both husbands I had dramatic arguments and romantic resolutions. Our relationships were dramatic, enthralling, and exciting.

My relationships with them were precisely imagined. One day, with age, I stopped fantasizing and moved onto real relationships.

Now, an adult by most definitions, I have an active imagination. I have a partner of three years. We've worked and traveled together. We've even lived together.

My future with him is precisely imagined. We'll have two weddings: one in Canada and one in Mexico, for his extended family. He'll be a doctor while I'm a self-employed artist. The farmhouse I grew up in will be our summer home. We'll have two children and we'll adopt more. Our oldest daughter will be named Lauriana. She'll be named after his mother, Laura. We'll stay up late sitting at our kitchen table talking through our disagreements and finding solutions for the trials of raising children. Our relationship will be work, but loving and longstanding.

My future with him is precisely imagined. In reality, one day I'll move onto a real partnership – with or without him.

Jeanette, 24

R....

R. was my boyfriend of six months. We were 'going steady' back in the days when that was still the term used for exclusive dating! Being of the 'Love, Sex, and Rock'n'Roll" generation, we were sleeping together several times a day. (Yes, R. was a randy lad and I was only too happy to oblige!) On his invitation, I attended a Graduate Student party at one of the more snobbish Eastern Ontario bastions of higher learning where we were both in attendance. I was in my early twenties, and damn good-looking, if not conventionally pretty. He was handsome and turned heads wherever we went. He was also very extroverted. I was quiet, smiled a lot, listened a lot, and said little. I was a good listener, so every male in the room with a big ego considered me to be an excellent conversationalist.

Unfortunately, there was a surfeit of big egos there that night. As I was scouting out the veggie tray, a drop dead gorgeous Middle-Eastern male with impeccable manners sought me out. We began chatting, and I soon learned that he had been a prince in his country of origin before the rebels rose up and threw him and his family unceremoniously out of power. Now he was a refugee and a graduate student, penniless but proud. He asked me if I was single, and I told him that I was there with my steady boyfriend. He immediately asked if he could speak to my boyfriend. Thinking nothing of it, I sought out R. who was surrounded (as usual) by a bevy of adoring females. R. came readily to meet the prince – not that R. was interested in princes; R. was in fact a fervent socialist. But he was interested in learning about conditions in the prince's former country, and who better than an eyewitness to describe the situation. The prince, however, had other ideas. He had no hesitation about coming straight to the point.

"Is this woman your woman?" the prince asked R.

I was not sure how I had suddenly gone from J. to "this woman," and was completely taken aback by the question. R. informed the prince that I was indeed his girlfriend. The prince then continued speaking to R. as though I had suddenly become invisible.

191

"I would like to spend the night with your woman," the prince stated bluntly. "Would this be acceptable to you?"

I hoped that R. would thereupon punch His Royal Highness (hereafter HRH) in his snooty nose, but no such luck. R. was, after all, not only a socialist but a budding feminist.

"It has nothing to do with me," R. informed HRH. "She is her own woman. Ask her."

And with that, R. pissed off! He left me standing there open-mouthed, a mistress of my own destiny. And who said that I wanted to be mistress of my own destiny? I wanted to see chivalry in action, damn it! Was chivalry dead along with the bourgeois establishment?

"Well, my dear?" HRH asked with a seductive smile.

He was so confident that I would accept. He was the sun and I was... I dread to think what I was. At any rate, I was one pissed off hippie chick!

"Fuck you!" I told HRH with a beatific smile, "and fuck you too!" I yelled at R. as I stormed out of the room. HRH looked absolutely crestfallen, but it took him about thirty seconds maximum to find another attractive female to chat up. As for R., he just laughed at my predicament. He found it funny, the bastard!

Afterwards, when I had calmed down enough not to punch R. out, we discussed the situation. It seems that R. thought that I would want to make that decision myself. Now R. knew that I was 100% faithful to him and head-over-heels in love with him to boot, so there was no chance that I was going to say 'yes' to HRH. I told R. that I would have appreciated a violent reaction from him, or at least a firm NO, that would not be acceptable," if he insisted on being a gentleman and a pacifist. R. told me that would not have been a politically correct response. Fuck politically correct! A girl wants chivalry, not politics, correct or otherwise!

I would like to tell you that R. and I broke up that night but that would be telling a lie. Like the good hippie chick I was, I swallowed my disappointment, and soldiered on. He was my man, flawed or otherwise. It wasn't until years later that I realized that R.'s response, in its own way, had been as insulting as HRH's question. R. meant well. But that night, his desire to be politically correct above righteously indignant sucked the big one, and left me feeling totally unprotected. (All right, all right, I wasn't big on feminism, okay?) Although we stayed together, I was never ever sure that he treasured me as a beloved woman should be treasured. It left me with a basic insecurity about the nature of our relationship. R. and I stayed together for several years, thereafter. We even moved in together, and eventually married, and eventually divorced. But never again, since that ill-fated night, was R. my knight in shining armor. I suppose it would not have bothered him. He never saw anything good about the feudal era with its gross inequalities and rampant injustice! But it bothered me. A girl, even a hippy chick, likes a little romance in her life.

Anonymous, 52

Rob....

I was finishing up a meal with my niece at Kelsey's, when I just happened to look up and meet eyes with a guy I had not seen for at least thirteen years. At 15, I had been totally in love with Rob. Well, at least what you would call 'love' at 15. Without hesitation, Rob came over to our table and greeted me. We were both smiling and ended up sitting really close together. It was as though we had never been apart. He told me that he was leaving for Australia and would be gone for three months! I immediately said that I did not want him to leave me now that I had found him again. I had thought he was married and living in Victoria, B.C. and researching whales. Instead, it turned out that he lived less then a ten-minute drive away and had been single for a year! He asked for my email address so that he could stay in touch with me.

Later that night, I went to the bar where he worked to have a farewell drink with him, but I did not have the opportunity to tell him how much he meant to me. The following afternoon, I went over to his place to say goodbye. He told me that he was happy to have found me again, and then he proceeded to tell me that he remembered me as a young girl, but now I was a beautiful woman. He told me that he had often thought about me and wondered what I was up to now. He confessed that he had feelings for me back then, but was not ready to explore them with me or to have somebody love him as I had loved him. He left me gasping and speechless. I could not believe what I was hearing. Out of the blue, he leaned over and kissed me. He said that he wanted to test the waters to see if there was anything there. There was something there alright.

Then Rob told me that he was ready to share his life with somebody and that he was tired of being single. I felt exactly the same way. That afternoon I learned that we both wanted similar things out of life, and I came away feeling that we could have a future together. As the afternoon progressed, his kisses became more and more intense. We ended up packing up his fridge and taking the cold food over to his parents' place. I was a little nervous meeting his parents, but it turned out that we all got along famously. We talked a lot about their past travels in Australia. Rob was conceived in Australia, but not born there, hence his strong pull to the land down under. We spent a good hour talking to his parents before heading back to his place.

At his place we put in a movie and ate pizza. The room was dark and we sat close together. When he started kissing me again, I suggested we make our way to someplace where there was more space. Naturally he complied, and we went to his bedroom. The rest of the night was amazing. Our entire minds, bodies and souls connected to the point where it was almost magical. It was like 'the first time' for both of us. We lost track of time and melted into each other's arms and eventually fell asleep. The next day, he left for Australia.

For the fun of it, I added Rob to my MSN messenger list, and was extremely surprised to find that he had been online and missed me. He left me a message to let me know that he loved me and was thinking of me. Over the next six weeks, Rob and I frequently met up online by pre-arrangement or by chance. Rob told me many times that he was a strong believer in fate, and that his meeting me at Kelsey's after all those years apart was meant to be. He said that he wanted to have a life with me when he returned to Canada. He told me that I was the one for him and that when the time was right, we would get engaged. It would be a short engagement of six or eight months! I thought that was taking things a little fast, but Rob convinced me that he loved me more than he had ever loved anyone else, and that he was ready to join his life with mine. He said that he wanted to write his own wedding vows because he didn't want anybody else telling him how he felt. He wanted to look in my eyes and speak words from his heart and soul and see my reaction.

I can hardly wait until Rob returns from Australia. We

have already discussed much of what we want in our lives, and yet we have so much left to learn about each other. Now it is only four weeks until his return, and I can't wait to see him! Are our hearts still in unity? I suppose only time and God know for sure, but for me, this is a fairytale romance that is just beginning...

Monique, 33

Ricardo....

Always follow your gut. It will never fail you. If it's too good to be true, it probably is. I met the man of my dreams, or at least I thought I did. I still remember one month into our relationship, things were amazing. I couldn't believe how perfect this new guy was for me. But for some reason, one sunny Sunday afternoon, I sat on the edge of his bed and got a shiver down my spine. He asked me if I was okay. I just looked up at him and blurted out, "You're going to break my heart." He lifted my chin, looked me directly in the eyes and said, "I promise, I'll never do anything to hurt you."

I should have followed my gut. Instead, I feel as though I wasted almost three years of my life. If a man wants to be with you he will do everything in his power to be with you. You live and you learn, I guess. If something doesn't feel right, it probably isn't. Take it from someone who learned the hard way!

Dinah, 27

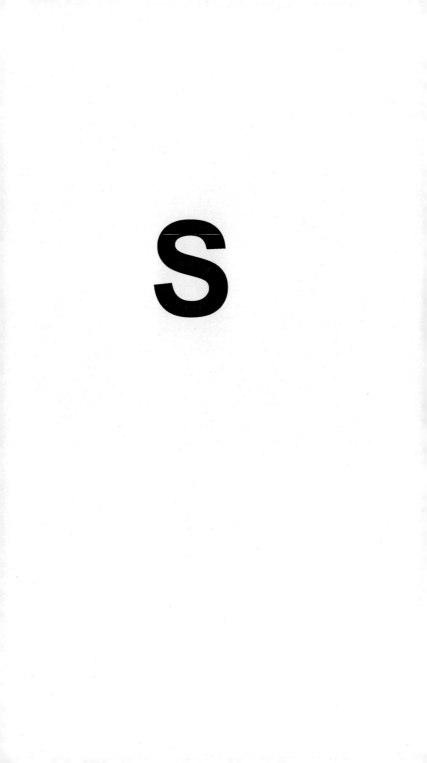
S

Steven....

You know you are in dating trouble when your first post-divorce interaction with a male, who is not a friend, takes place in Canadian Tire on a busy Saturday morning. You have dropped most of your items on the floor and this really hot guy 10 years your junior picks one item up and says, "Screw?"

Heather, 46

Simon....

Simon arrived on campus in the second year of my music degree. He was the new 'hot guy' in the department, a singer from the States who was taking lessons and doing solo gigs before returning to Philadelphia to do his Masters. He certainly was cute, but what all the girls who lusted after him didn't realize – but I eventually did being the 'lucky' girl he went after – was that he was also self-centered, egotistical and stupid. In hindsight, it served me right for dating a tenor, who are infamous for having big egos. But I was about ten years younger and thirty years more naïve than I am today. His favourite topics of conversation included talking about what great blue eyes he had and how he was going to be a star. His moods were entirely dependent on how well he sang that day. If people praised his talent, all was fine. But even the smallest piece of criticism would send him into a depression.

In retrospect, it was not a happy or healthy relationship, but at the time I was crazy about him and felt lucky to be his girl. However, after eight months of ignoring my gut feeling that I had to get out of the relationship, he dumped me. I was devastated (although to this day I'm not sure if I was truly heartbroken or if my ego was just bruised and I was mad at myself for not giving him the boot first). But now I can say thank goodness for the guys who break your heart early on. They have the potential to teach you so much, including all the bad behaviour that you are not willing to put up with.

Simon taught me that when you date a frog – even if everyone tells you how lucky you are to be dating a prince – you're still stuck with a frog. He taught me that it's better to be single than to be in a relationship with someone whose histrionics drain you of all your energy. And he taught me to trust my gut because when you truly listen to your instincts, they will never lead you in the wrong direction.

Kathryn, 32

Scott....

It was his eyes, bright, shining and an electric shade of blue unlike anything I had ever seen, which first caught my attention. He sat next to me in my second year World Politics class and I couldn't have him. Not because he wasn't interested, but because he was. He stole my pen, drew in my book and pinched me during class. No, this was not grade one. We were two 20 year-old university students, adult for the most part, or as much of an adult as you can be at 20. I couldn't have him because I was in love with someone else. At least I thought I was.

How we got where we are today is long and messy, but what part of life isn't? The important thing is that he turned out to be the most real thing in my life, teaching me what love is and what love should be. Complicated and frustrating some days, but magical and worth all of the bumps, bruises, and broken hearts before him. Our relationship is not perfect, it's not always organized, neat and tidy the way I like my life to be (he leaves his dirty socks everywhere BUT the laundry hamper). But what I have learned is this: It doesn't matter. None of the small stuff is important. When I wake up beside him in the morning, the only thing I care about is sharing my life with him, dirty socks and all.

Michelle, 24

Steve....

I'm 22 and in this relationship with a hot guy who is four years older than me. He is totally set up with his own downtown loft, an Audi TT, and a wicked travel schedule. At the time he was my dream guy. He had been around the world, started a couple of cool 'dot coms', and had been unattached until I came into the picture.

At the beginning of the relationship I remember going to all these parties and having people say, "What? Steve has a girlfriend???!". I was flattered and I felt special to be the one that he chose to present as his girlfriend after a period of self-declared bachelorhood. I was the girl that everyone wanted to meet.

A couple of months passed and I started to spend more time at his place. At dinner one night he casually complimented me on my new Gucci handbag (which *is* gorgeous). Later that evening I was watching TV back at his loft and I had to go to the bathroom. As I passed his bedroom I caught a glimpse of Steve trying on my Gucci purse while posing in the mirror. It was so bizarre that I pretended not to see a thing and I walked quickly past the bedroom door and straight to the bathroom. While I was in there I was thinking, "Oh my God, he's gay." It all made sense. The purse pose, the genuine shock from his friends when they met me, the self-declared bachelorhood...

Seven years later and I'm still not convinced otherwise. As far as I know, Steve is living status quo. Hmmmmmmmm...

Anne, 28

Sean....

Until I met Sean, I didn't believe in soul mates. I've never had a connection with anyone like that before or after him. Then I lost him.

We met on a flight out of LA. He was on his way to visit his grandparents in Toronto and I was returning home. Instantly I felt comfortable with him, like we'd known each other our whole lives. We chatted the whole flight and watched the sunset. He wrote me a poem. It was a spectacular and moving five hours. We exchanged contact info but somehow I lost his. I still remember sitting with my girlfriends months after that listening to music and talking about past loves. If love at first sight exists, this was it. Only time and fate will tell.

I wonder what he's up to now...

Dinah, 27

Steve....

I had just finished my second year in the Journalism program at Humber College. I moved to Collingwood for the summer to stay with my mother, something I did every year around June. Collingwood was my escape. The recent abrupt ending in May with an on-going fling left me bitter, angry, and craving the carefree days that only a summer in Collingwood and nights at Wasaga Beach could provide. But, like many other women my age, I had also gotten caught up in the whole online dating craze. If I couldn't find any good men back home to treat me right, there had to be one floating around in the shadows of some online dating community that would.

Lesson I should have learned by now is that guys you meet online are no different than guys you meet at bars or any other location.

I received a message from someone that went by the handle XL-DJK. I was shocked. I stared wide-eyed at the picture of this man, nestled between the arms of a real tiger at some convention in downtown Toronto. Were my eyes deceiving me? Or was it Steve? A couple emails later it was confirmed that XL-DJK was, infact, Steve, and before I knew it we were talking like we had been best friends forever. This was also when I told him I had a crush on him in high school. You see, Steve was my first high-school crush. We had never spoken at school, but his leather-jacket wearing, pretty boy looks made my heart race whenever I saw him in the halls. He was loud, funny and obnoxious, and I ate it up. He had been kicked out of school before I graduated, and that was the last I ever saw of him.

Silver Lining

The next lesson I should have learned by now is: Never let a guy know you used to like him. It has bad news written all over it.

Of course, being the gullible idiot that I can sometimes be, I convinced myself that it was fate. I promptly took the next weekend off of work to go back home and see him, and we spent the night looking at old yearbooks while he rambled on about how he always thought I was hot and couldn't believe I never talked to him before. But I tuned him out. I was too busy thinking to myself how I couldn't be sitting here, in my apartment, with the guy that I had a crush on for so many years, that I thought never even knew my name. I'm not a religious person, but I thanked the Lord on several occasions that night. And no, we never did anything.

Next lesson: Talk is cheap.

We clicked so well that I seriously started believing that I had finally found "Mr. Right." I made the mistake of quitting work almost a month before I was scheduled to so that I could spend more time with him before school started. We would hang out almost every day. He would say the sweetest things to me over the phone and send random text messages that made me smile. We would do our grocery shopping together, attend each other's family functions, and he would help me with gas whenever we had errands to run. We would meet during the early hours of the morning for a coffee since both of us had trouble sleeping and a shared addiction to caffeine. I really started believing he wasn't just another asshole when he told me "I really like you, Ash, and I want us to take this slow because I always rush into things."

Through our conversations I had learned that he had recently gotten out of a two year relationship with a girl who cheated on him. This girl did the most despicable things to him, he told me. As the weeks went by, and we grew closer emotionally, it finally dawned on me that we hadn't even kissed yet. I would ask what the deal was, but all I would get was "patience is a virtue," and he would quickly change the subject. My friends and family started cautioning me, telling me that he was using me for money and rides so that he didn't have to take the bus anymore. He had been laid off from work a few months before we met.

If a guy can't buy his own toilet paper, you have a problem.

Clearly I wasn't going to believe anything that people were telling me because how could someone who says such sweet things, and does so much for me, be such a bad person. I ignored my inner voice and kept hoping for the best. I was even stupid enough to believe his story a couple months later that it was "his friend's girlfriend," when I caught him with another girl in his apartment, after he wouldn't open the door. He finally got a new job, and being the moron that I was at the time, I offered to drive him to work – which then turned into me driving him there and picking him up every day. If I couldn't he'd lay the guilt trip on thick.

More weeks went by and I started catching him lying about the stupidest things. Our disagreements were no longer disagreements – they were full fledged vocal outbursts that involved him throwing things around and screaming until his neighbours knocked on the door. One night, while throwing out my Kleenex in his garbage, I noticed something odd sitting on top – a used condom. His excuse this time was every time he had to – how do I put this? – pleasure himself, his cats would sniff around the mess, so a condom was the cleanest, most logical answer. I'm ashamed to admit I actually bought that story. But deep down I knew the truth. I was stupid and didn't want to admit I was being played. There were no good days after that incident.

Silver Lining

It finally came to an end on St. Patrick's Day, 2005. We did our own thing that night, and at 2:00 a.m. I received a call on my cell phone from his best friend, telling me to come pick him up at the local pizza place because he was drunk and they didn't want to deal with him. I went and when I arrived, an intoxicated Steve met me at the door, stumbling and slurring and spilling pizza sauce everywhere. He was a far cry from the pretty boy I adored in high school. He asked me what I was doing there and before I had a chance to answer, he was slamming me into the side of my car, screaming at me for "following him." I cried, he yelled more, his friend tried to pull him off me, they threw punches, jackets were ripped, pizza was flying out of his mouth at an incredible rate – it was a horrible scene. Then just as quickly as it began, it ended, and he ran off down the road towards his apartment. I was now sitting in my car, crying uncontrollably. He had repeatedly slammed the door on my leg while I was trying to get away from him. His friend opened the door and hugged me until I stopped. He then confirmed all the suspicions I had about Steve. Everything had been a lie. He never had a girlfriend who cheated on him – he cheated on her – twice. The girl in his apartment was there with him, not his friend, and the used condom was compliments of his "good friend Claudia." He was using me and I knew it all along. I kicked myself for weeks afterwards for being so stupid and gullible. I did a bit of math, and in the eight months that I spent with him, not only had I succeeded in shafting all my friends, I spent upwards of $800 on him – not including the gas I used to get him to and from work every day.

The hot boys from high school can end up as violent alcoholics later on in life. Save yourself the trouble and get a crush on the geeky computer club president.

I won't go into detail about how later that night I made his friend go up to his apartment to get some stuff I had there, and we found him passed out in the elevator, still drunk, next to a puddle of his own piss – the elevator had gotten stuck when he pressed the emergency button instead of his floor. And I won't go into detail about how a few weeks after all this I ran into another friend of his I knew who informed me that Steve had been evicted from his apartment for not paying rent, and laid off from his job for stealing food out of the crates on the loading dock. And I definitely won't mention how when I drive by his parents place, on the way to my high-paying dream job, I see him sitting on the front porch, shirtless, beer belly hanging out for the entire world to see and with a look on his face that only a mother could love. I won't mention any of that. I think he's suffered enough, don't you?

Ashley, 22

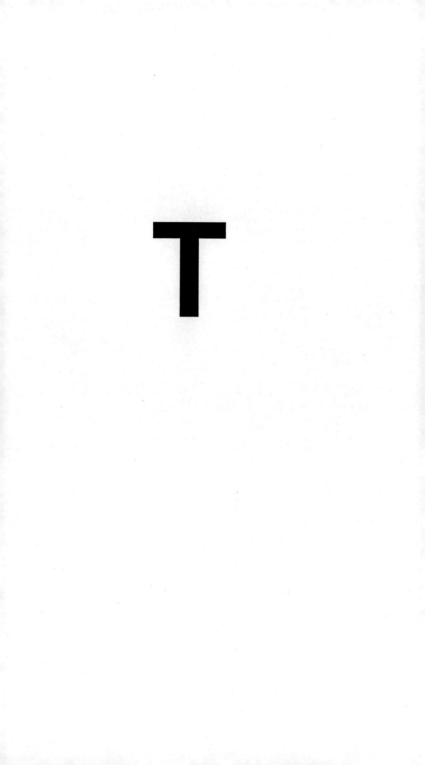

Testosterone....

Frazzled feeling threat
when the voice of Testosterone rises
and slings sharp arrows
from strings of words that sting and begin and end in
fuck—Fuck—FUCK—FUCK   What the FUCK?

Testosterone has a point to make
for me to hear
i listen   i stir   i try to speak.
Testosterone doesn't hear me or if he does he raises
his voice   slings his strings   and "Fuck"
i listen
i rub Testosterone's back
try to sooth   rub belly
wanting to understand
i become too willing
to forget
voice gets lost
i run ragged
trip
fall down
pick myself up
fall
get up
fall
rise
fall
hold onto my strings
speak
speak
silence
speak
silence
silence
speak
speak
silence

Silver Lining

silence
silence
silence
…

    …

        …

           …

depression
again   Testosterone has something to say and like a
crazed witch I stand in the middle of the room
I pull my own hair and I can't stand up straight because
words come from my diaphragm causing me to bend at
the waist and the knees my stomach is tight muscles
and veins pop words are vomit I spew
I spit out toxic waste speaking his language saying
FUCK YOU! WHAT ABOUT ME?

Edith, 40

Trent….

The Knife Man.

I had an interesting evening with Trent the Knife Man.
I hadn't seen him in months. Evenings with Trent are
always interesting if somewhat intense, which is
probably why I don't see him too often.

Trent is one of the most genuine people I have ever
met. Genuinely strange that is. I have memories of
Trent marching across the library lawns (although he
lopes more than marches) but whatever the proper
term, he always seems to cover a great deal of ground
with each stride.

Trent has always reminded me of a character out of a
Beano comic. I am not entirely sure what I mean by
that, seeing as I haven't even seen a Beano comic for

212

the last decade or so but I think it's that the Beano Characters that I remember have sort of crew-cut black hair, left to grow long at the back of the neck. Sort of like Sid Vicious with a mullet.

Trent wore acid washed jeans long before (and after) they were fashionable. He wore black boots with knives in them. Don't ask me exactly where in the boots these knives resided but he could always produce them on request or demand - hence his name the Knife Man. He was usually in the process of handling some weapon or other. I met him at a karate class.

The most fascinating thing about Trent is that it's impossible to offend him. And believe me I have tried everything. He can be so irritating that there are times when I would have liked nothing better than to take repeated swings at him and the only reason I have resisted any expressions of violence is because he would have felt no pain, only satisfaction at having got a rise out of me. In a way it is nice to know that I can't offend him because it makes me free of being responsible for his feelings or his happiness. On the other hand, it can be incredibly frustrating because I am not able to dent him.

Trent is a drug-taking, weapons-dealing, punk-drumming engineer. I know - I usually steer clear of engineers. For Trent I make an exception because he gives a great massage. He is the most generous person in the galaxy when it comes to massages. One time he spent four hours massaging me.

However, with Trent there is no such thing as a simple, traditional massage. Once, after massaging me, he informed me that he had programmed me to sexually attack some lucky male and that the passion I would feel would be like nothing I have ever felt before. Needless to say, I was self-disciplined enough to not let this occur; forewarned is forearmed I always like to say but I also have to be honest enough to admit that no such opportunity presented itself to me in any case.

There was another time Trent was massaging me, and I was entirely relaxed, wallowing in the attention. I felt a sharp, cold, feathery lightness moving across my lower back. I looked up sleepily and there was Trent holding a large knife, a sort of hunting knife with scalloped edges on the one side.

"Don't move like that again," he said. "Or I could cut you by mistake." I lay down and didn't move a muscle.

There was a time when my mother thought that Trent was a suitable candidate for a serious relationship. She went on and on about how nice he seemed. Eventually I had to combat that Mother-knows-best wisdom and I was forced to share some truth with her.

"Mom, all Trent wants to do is handcuff me to the bed."

So now whenever I mention him she disapprovingly refers to him as "that sick person."

I couldn't remember why I hadn't seen him in ages but in an effort to fill up my calendar I phoned him.

"Trent, my life is so boring right now that I am phoning to tell you to take me out. Entertain me, show me some fun and above all, do not involve me in any of the decision-making processes! Instruct me – direct me!"

"I am honoured and privileged," he said. "I will call you back with The Plan." I waited, expecting a list of low dives and trips to dangerous places from which I might not escape unscathed.

"Ballet," said Trent. "Don Quixote followed by dinner."

Hmmm. Unexpected. But I was game to go along with the plan since things were very rarely usual with Trent. Ballet was great and dinner was good. I was enjoying flirting with the guy over Trent's left shoulder who was obviously enjoying looking at me.

"The guy over my left shoulder," said Trent, "find a way to get him to ask you for your phone number. But you can't just give it to him. He has to ask you. If you don't achieve this, you lose."

"I lose what?" I asked

"Your honour," he said.

I distracted him from this impossible mission by showing him how my expressions were coming along. He said my impression of shy and virginal was excellent, that my distressed needed work (I fidgeted too much), my interested looked bland, and my dumb blonde was superb. Trent will discuss me for hours, which is another reason why I like seeing him.

We discussed how stressed I was, how tired, how overworked. I told him how I wouldn't go out anywhere unless there was a way for me to leave, be it by car or money for a plane ticket. I had to be able to leave. I asked Trent if this made me a claustrophobic or an agoraphobic. He said it made me a brat. We went home and Trent massaged me for hours. He massaged me until I fell asleep. He massaged me until I woke up and fell asleep again. I didn't even remember him leaving.

I have no idea what he had programmed me for this time, but his massage had made me feel full of wound up energy. I wondered if perhaps I should indeed have a deep and meaningful relationship with him.

I really thought that I might but then he phoned me

three days in a row. Conversing for three days in a row? Who had that much to say? My anxiety about his ever-increasing presence in my life realized itself when I ate half a trifle. I realized it was because he was putting pressure on me to commit.

I am definitely going to have to avoid him again for a while.

Lisa, 27

Timothy....

I was one of those women who always ended up with the wrong guy. They all seemed unable to commit and unable to be monogamous. I was forever having my heart broken. My ex-husband had several affairs during our marriage, as did my fiancée after him. I spent all my energy trying to fix their problems and help them realize what real love could be like.

Utter exhaustion finally made me change my ways. I just no longer had the energy or the inclination to fix anybody. I started focusing on myself, and what I wanted in my life. I stopped thinking that I needed a man. In fact, I stopped even wanting one. I came to the conclusion that I would be okay if I remained single the rest of my life, I would be A-okay with that. In fact, I learned I quite enjoyed my own company. Wouldn't you know it; at that exact period in my life I met my current husband (who is 7 years my junior I might add). He was 24, I was 31. We have now been together close to six years (married two) and have a 20-month-old daughter. He is completely faithful and loyal. While he may not be perfection incarnate, he loves me to the tips of his toes.

Connie, 37

Tony….

Tony and I were already pretty serious by our first Christmas. We had discussed our future on several occasions and I truly thought, "He could be 'The One'." I helped him pick out gifts for all his family members including his Grandma. For his Grandma we decided on a wool cardigan sweater. It was the kind of sweater that made me itch just looking at it but it was a good grandma sweater. On Christmas morning I unwrapped my gift from Tony. It was the Grandma sweater! We broke up by New Years.

Susan, 25

Ted….

Ted was at the Grey Cup game in Toronto. I was in the airport lounge watching the Grey Cup game waiting for a connector flight to Edmonton. An hour after the game ended I was boarding the flight. That is when Ted says he first noticed me.

I got settled in my seat when a very confused man asked if the empty seat beside me was 18A "Yes", I replied, "It must be, I am in 18B." After asking me a couple more times if I was sure, I managed to convince him that it was indeed 18A. Now I know now that Ted was confused because he had asked for a non-smoking seat, but had been sat in the smoking section (beside the woman he had noticed earlier in the airport). As he attempted to put his carry on in the overhead bin I warned him not to open the bin directly above his head because there was a fur coat in it and it would fall on his head. I knew this because it had already fallen on mine. Again he looked confused and obviously not believing me he opened the bin and the coat fell on his head. As he struggled to get the coat in the bin and close it before it fell out again, I was wondering if he was disoriented or just not all that bright.

We started talking. He traveled a lot. He had arranged to be in Toronto on Friday so he could be at the game Sunday, He had to be in Vancouver on Monday afternoon, so he was flying back to Edmonton to unpack and repack. We worked in the same industry and knew some of the same people. He was extremely personable and very easy to talk to so I should have been impressed, but I worked with sales people and I knew how much training they had to come across this way. I saw most of it as being phony, something he had learned in some marketing course somewhere, so I was not impressed. But we had a lot of fun and had drank way to much Kaluha and coffee by the end of the flight. The stewardesses parked the cart by us and told us to help ourselves. He traveled a lot, he knew the stewardesses by name and they all seemed to like him. Again, maybe I should have been impressed but I saw this as a man playing a role. Although I did drink the free Kaluha.

My sister picked me up from the airport and we offered to give him a ride home, which he accepted. The next day I received flowers at work and a note saying how much he enjoyed his flight home the day before. I should have been impressed, but I saw it as being a little too smooth. He probably read that in *How to Win Friends and Influence People*. I didn't believe it to be genuine. He phoned me late in the day at work (because I hadn't given him my home number) and I thanked him for the flowers. After we chatted for a while he asked me if I would go to his company Christmas party on the weekend. I had been in that position before, scrambling for a date for a Christmas party or a wedding. My compassion kicked in and I said yes. People didn't tell me I was a nice person for nothing!

He arrived on time and was very complimentary. We had fun over dinner but I had judged him to be phony so I didn't really give him much of a chance. The dance started and I didn't see him again all night. Every one of his co-worker's wives was asking him to dance or engaging him in conversation. All the women seemed to love him! As I sat there by myself an older gentleman came over and struck up a conversation. He found out I was Ted's date and proceeded to tell me what I nice guy he was. I told him I thought his personality was a little phony and I didn't trust that he was sincere. Percy spent the next hour convincing me that what I saw was real and Ted really was kind, considerate and sincere. By the time we left the Christmas party that night I was looking at Ted through new eyes, thanks to Percy.

The rest is history. We were married two years later and we now have four wonderful children together. All of those things that I was too quick to judge I have learnt are not only sincere in Ted, but are exemplary. I am impressed with how personable, honest and caring he is. I am impressed with his sense of humor. I am impressed with how much he respects women and how easily he gets along with them and appreciates them. I am impressed with his sincerity and genuine kindness, his continuous generosity and his total dedication to me and our family. He has been the biggest blessing in my life. He is the kindest, most thoughtful man I know, a little quirky at times but still a fantastic husband and father. We will be celebrating our 25th Anniversary in 2006 and still love and respect each other very much.

Lorrette, 49

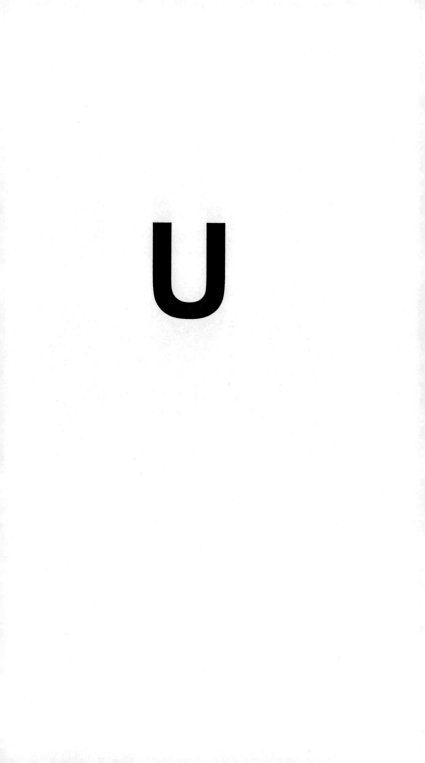

U

Uri....

Uri is an exchange student at my school. He was only in Canada for one month but as soon as we met, we really liked each other. We hung out every day after school and when he left I felt heartbroken. Everyone told me that I was too young to fall in love and that I didn't understand how I felt. I disagree. I do know that I loved Uri. I know that I miss him and can't do anything to be with him. Older people have it easy – they can find the money or time to go see someone, even if they are far away. I am stuck missing him with no chance to make the situation better. I wanted to write my story to remind everyone that love is not restricted to age. Love is a feeling – and anyone can experience feelings.

Stephanie, 15

Ugo....

I worked for a national marketing company and had been at a training event in Toronto. One of the other staff members and I hung out a bit, but nothing to write home about. Two months later I got a surprise on my front door step. He had flown to Edmonton to see me and thought I would be thrilled to see him. Of course, he stayed with me – where was I going to send him? I was literally the only person he knew in Edmonton. It was a weekend from hell. We had nothing to say to each other and he kept trying to make things physical, which was definitely not going to happen. He even went to so far as to tell me that he had make-out buddies in lots of cities, and he would be totally okay with me being his make-out buddy in Edmonton.
Wow – thanks.

Sandra, 48

Urbain....

Urbain and I met one night at a bar.

For about four months we would be in touch intermittently. The entire time we were in touch, he never once called me. He text-messaged me every time. I would even tell him in a text message to call me, and he would text back his response. I would call him, he wouldn't answer, but would text message me later after listening to the message.

Apparently new technology provides men with even more extreme ways to be non-committal. Like they needed any more!

Isabelle, 37

Vaughn....

April of 1998:
I performed in a musical. I was a 'Neighbor Dancer.'

July of 2000:
I was in a bar and walking from the bathroom back to my friends when someone grabbed my arm. He told me he "knew me" and I thought it was some lame pick-up line. After trying to convince him that we did not know each other for a couple of minutes, he was still holding onto my arm. He started asking questions. He asked if I had danced. I said yes, but not for a couple of years. Then he asked if I acted. I gave him the same response. Then he asked if I had been involved in a production in 1998. I said yes, and then felt bad that I hadn't recognized him (thinking he must have been in it too). But he hadn't, and he was still holding my arm. I turned to walk away but his grip tightened. All of a sudden he said, "Jane, I know you." Again, trying to walk away I said, "No, you don't." Then he said, "Yes, I do. You were a Neighbor Dancer and I saw you in the performance on April 18, 1998. I was sitting in Row X, Seat 26. I saw you in the first scene and I couldn't keep my eyes off of you the entire time." I told him that was totally crazy and there was no way he could remember me from that experience, with stage make up and lights... besides, I was two years older. I looked entirely different. He went on to tell me that he knew we were meant to be together and that he would leave his girlfriend for me. I got freaked out, yanked my arm away and left the bar immediately.

December 2000:
I was at my church when I noticed a guy walk in and sit right behind me. He looked familiar but I couldn't place why. After church I was walking when all of a sudden someone grabbed my arm. I instantly felt nervous and scared, but had no idea why. It was the oddest

sensation. This guy asked me if I remembered him. Feeling bad, I told him that he looked familiar, but I couldn't place why. He said, "Jane, it is me, Vaughn, from Canada Day." I just about had a heart attack. I started shaking. Again, he wouldn't let go of my arm. I made some comment about it being a really weird coincidence that he happened to be at the same church as me. He told me it wasn't a coincidence. Then he told me that he had found me. I tried to pull my arm away or grab someone's attention, but he wasn't letting go and no one was paying attention. I told him that I didn't want to talk to him and that I had to go. He told me that we were going out for dinner on Thursday night of that week. I told him that I was not interested and if he contacted me again I would call the police. He ignored me and went on to ask me if I had ever held a gun. He said he was going to take me to the shooting range. He told me that the feeling of power you have when you hold a gun is like nothing else I would ever experience. At this point I started to cry. I told him that the only thing I wanted to talk to him about was how he found me. He told me that he would tell me on Tuesday night when he called to confirm our date for Thursday night. Finally he left.

On Tuesday night he called. With my parents as witnesses, I told him that I was not interested in seeing him or talking to him again. He wanted to keep talking and I kept asking him how he found me, how he had my number, and why he was going to all this trouble. He wasn't giving me any information. When I was about to hang up he said he would tell me. He told me he saw me in the play, and then saw me over two years later in the bar and he got the same "feeling" that he had the first time he saw me. After I left the bar that night he went and talked to my friends, pretending he was an old friend who just noticed me leaving the bar and wanted to know what I was up to. They gave him a list of activities I was involved in and he started his search. One of the activities my friends told him I was involved in was church. He went to a different church every Sunday for 13 weeks, looking for people my age and asking them if they knew me and where I went to church. Finally he had succeeded. I told him that if I heard from him again I would put a restraining order on him and hung up the phone.

May 2001:
I had been on the radio promoting a charity event I was involved in. Part of the pitch was that we were looking for sponsorship money. I was getting a couple of letters a week with donations in them so when I received this one in particular, it didn't seem like a big deal. I opened it and read the traditional support letter. But then, the last paragraph threw me for a loop. It said, "And on a personal note, I just wanted to let you know that our whole family was devastated when you turned down Vaughn's invitation to go to the shooting range with him..." It went on to say that the entire family knew we were meant to be together and they all looked forward to the day when I realized that as well. It was signed by his mom.

I took the letter to the police. It wasn't until that point that I realized there was no stamp on it – meaning it had been hand delivered.

Now, it is September 2005 – over four years since I received that letter. I have only seen Vaughn once again. He was in a parking lot as I walked to my car but he didn't try to approach me. You hear stories of stalkers and you think that it doesn't happen to real people. But it does. It happened to me. Even as I sit here putting it down on paper and reliving the events, it makes my skin crawl. There is something extremely invasive about someone knowing information about you and using it to watch you. The questions around the whole situation were never really answered. Why did he even care? What triggered this? How many times was he around that I didn't see? Has he forgotten about me or will he show up again? It is extremely unsettling.

Yet, even with all the circumstances around it, I hesitated before going to the police. Everyone was pushing me to go but I couldn't. Looking back now I realize that because it meant so much to me, I was scared to death that I would go to the police and they would tell me that it wasn't a big deal. I was so worried about having my feelings invalidated that I almost overlooked my safety. When I went to the police, the officer on duty told me that my story was one of the creepiest ones he had heard in a long time. They gave Vaughn a formal warning and put me into a Victim Protection program for three months.

Trust your gut. If you are in a situation in your life that feels uncomfortable or not right, it most likely isn't. The whole situation gave me a new sympathy and understanding of why girls who have been abused don't always go to the police. Although I was never actually abused, the feelings you deal with when you feel like someone has come uninvited into your world leave you feeling extremely vulnerable. To know there is a chance that someone will tell you that your feelings are wrong, or that there is nothing they can do for you, is devastating.

That being said, please take this story as a reminder that your safety is in your hands. If there is something going on in your life or someone who needs to be held accountable for his or her actions, take a step to protect yourself and stop this person from causing any more harm to you or others.

Jane, 23

Victor....

Inside Out...

The last year has been a roller coaster of emotions for me. My husband and I separated after being together twenty years. When I moved away it felt like it wasn't real, that I was in a daze. I would never do something like this!

I loved my husband. We had beautiful, healthy children, a nice home – everything you wish for. So, why was I so unhappy? Our relationship had faded to two people living in the same house, watching television, and not having much to say. We didn't do much together and I was tired of trying to make the relationship work, of trying to be happy. I felt my husband didn't love me enough. What I now realize is that it wasn't that he didn't love me enough but that the love he gave me was all he was able to give, and I wanted more. Regardless of how we ended up apart, it happened.

In the beginning it didn't feel real. It felt like I was just away on a trip. And then reality hit. He didn't love me and he didn't want me back. He had replaced me with another woman. To him it was over, no looking back. He filled the void because he couldn't be alone. I had hurt him too badly.

Then my depression set in, the millions of tears I cried, the real feelings of being alone; the rejection I felt, the resentment that I had because of his relationship with this new woman, and the jealousy I felt because she had my husband. These feelings consumed me for months and at times I still feel the pain. But I am working at getting rid of these feelings. It's funny to think I was with this person almost half of my life and now I wonder - were we ever really friends? Were we

231

really in love? These are questions that won't ever be answered.

With the love and the support of my daughters and my friends my life is certainly looking brighter. Being happy sure feels good, and the happy days are now out-numbering the sad days. I still have a very long road of healing ahead of me. I now understand the importance of giving yourself the time to heal. Then, when you least expect it, something wonderful will happen to you. I know the road I travel is still going to be bumpy at times, and likely have some unexpected turns, but that's the adventure I have to look forward to. I've stepped off the roller coaster of emotion. I no longer feel inside out.

Lynn, 46

Wyatt....

When I was in university I had a guy come to pick me up for our first date with four dead coyotes in the back of his truck. He must have thought he could 'Wow' me with his hunter-and-gatherer skills. Needless to say, that was our only date.

Anonymous

Walker....

I grew up in a very small town. There were the 'cool' girls and the 'not cool' girls. I, unfortunately, was 'not cool.' When I was a young teen the *New Kids on the Block* were going to be performing in the nearest city center. Some of the cool girls were organizing a bus to go to the concert and I reserved tickets for myself and a friend. After confirming that we had tickets, we showed up at the bus, ready to go to the concert, only to be told by these girls that they had not gotten us any tickets. We were devastated. My mom was a hero that day and drove us into the city and found tickets. She only bought two, as she couldn't afford anything more, and sat in the car for the entire night waiting for us while we enjoyed the concert.

Years later I was back at home visiting my parents. I happened to go out to the only local bar one night and it was one of the 'cool' girls birthday party at the bar. Still bitter about the whole event (yes, even though it was six years later), I noticed that her long time crush, Walker, was there. Walker was the one guy that she could never get and it killed her. Walker and I were good friends, so I made sure we were extra chummy that night. At the end of the night, after I made sure she was watching, I left with Walker and lost my virginity to him, just to spite her.

I found out recently that the 'cool girl' and Walker are now married! Oops!

Reese, 29

Warren....

I am a trillion miles from home. The man who has been my soulmate since I was 18 years-old is speaking to me on the phone. He tells me I don't need a piece of paper to tell me how I feel; I realize the distance is final. In Toronto, on a counter, in the house I now share with two wonderful women, is the envelope with the papers that prove this is true.

When we separated, friends actually cried. The completeness we radiated to the world for thirteen years had been real. But there is a reason why fairy tales end at the start of the relationship. At thirty-two, on a bleak December morning with a rented van and three friends, I left my marriage. I don't want to go back, but I have never completely left.

Heather, 46

Xavier....

Actual Conversation...

"Hi, my name is Xavier."

"Hi Xavier, I'm Karen."

"How are you?"

"Fine, thanks."

"What time do you get off work today?"

"Six."

"Well, when you are done, do you want to go out for some soup?"

"Huh?"

Karen, 28

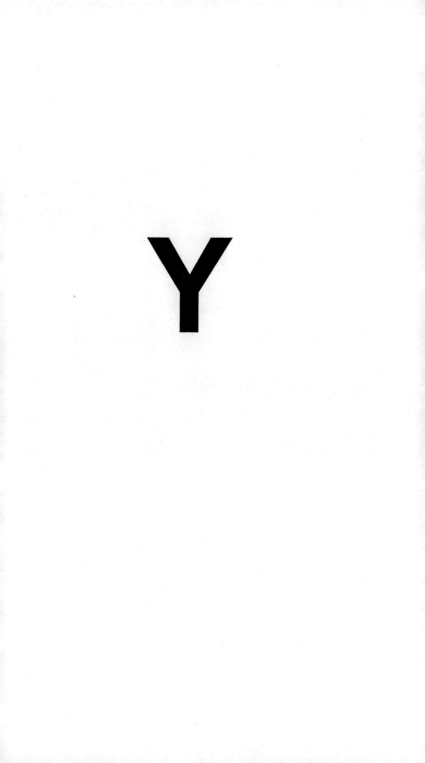

Yan....

I went on my first date when I was 14. We went to a movie, and then out for some pizza. I remember this date vividly fourteen years later, not because it was my first date, but because he had a booger the size of my fist hanging out of his nose the entire time!

Christine, 28

Yuri....

According to Judaism, forty days before I was born, a heavenly proclamation declared the person I was destined to be with. At 33 and single, I find this comforting. This idea of soul mates, of your one true destined love, and the knowledge that all the times it didn't work out - blind dates, Internet dates, set-ups, speed-dating, singles events - were part of the heavenly proclamation. You name it, I've done it. And somehow, I haven't given up hope.

The first blind date I had was with the brother of a friend's friend. I was 24, a year out of university, and living on my own in my first apartment. We were set up by mutual friends, liked each other, and agreed to meet again. We began dating and had been dating for two months when I invited him to join me in Waterloo for Oktoberfest celebrations with my university friends. Oktoberfest is an excuse to drink exorbitant amounts of beer, and this year was no exception. Everyone was drunk. Two hours into the evening, after many beers, my friend Mike came up to me.

"Lisa, Dave is picking fights with all of our friends and hitting on all the girls. You better go talk to him."

Silver Lining

I went to look for him, but I couldn't find him anywhere. Then the DJ found me.

"Lisa, you need to go outside right now. The cops have Dave."

I went running out the front door. Dave was face down on the ground, with a cop's knee in his back holding him there.

He was yelling at the cops, "You can't keep me here. You have no right to do this to me. I know my rights!"

"Dave, just shut up and go with them," I pleaded.

They finally pushed him into the car.

"Officer, can you tell me what's happening here? Where are you taking him?"

"He's been arrested for public drunkenness, and we're taking him to the drunk tank for the evening. Here's the information on where you can call and pick him up."

I picked him up the next morning at 6 a.m. and we drove back to Toronto in silence. When I dropped him off, he said, "I'll understand if you don't want to see me again." And that was the end of that.

I met Mitch at a Jewish singles event, a Friday night Shabbat dinner. We connected and were enjoying spending time together. At the end of the night, he asked for my number. We started dating and had been dating for two months when a few strange things happened. Mostly I chose to ignore them. For example, he took home a doggie bag every single time we went to dinner. At the beginning of the night, as soon as his food arrived at the table, he'd exclaim, "Oh good, I'll have enough food to take home." Then one night at dinner, he emptied a sugar packet on the table. He proceeded to lick his finger, put his finger to the sugar, and then bring his finger to his mouth in order to consume the sugar. However, the strangest event occurred one night at my apartment while we were sitting watching TV - I looked over and he had his penis in his hand. Yes, that's right. His penis. He was holding onto it. He wasn't doing anything to it. But he was holding on to it. "What are you doing?" I asked.

"What?" he replied. "Who cares if I want to hold onto it?"

And that was the end of that.

Then I tried 'The Book.' The Book was a dating service located in the library of the local synagogue. The book contained pictures and profiles of potential 'soul mates.' You choose someone who interested you and then you then filled out a postcard indicating that you were interested in meeting this person. The synagogue sent the postcard to your love interest in the mail. You would then go into the synagogue to look up the person's profile, and if you liked what you saw, you would call them. This was only three years ago, but imagine such physical labour when all you have to do now is go online for a few minutes! I noticed Howie's profile in the book and sent him a card. Howie responded. We went to dinner. The date was good. I waited for Howie to call. He never did. A month later, my friend Tara (who was also in the book) said to me, "Lisa, Howie sent me a card. Do you mind if I go out with him?"
"Of course not. We only had one date." Tara and Howie went out. And then they went out again.
And then again. And then they got married. And that was the end of that.

Then there was Steve whom I met at synagogue. Nice man. Committed to Judaism and to his family. Shy. Awkward. But sweet and kind. We had four dates and he still hadn't kissed me. One night he was at my apartment for dessert and coffee. I couldn't take it any longer.

"Are you ever going to kiss me?" I asked.

As he choked and spit out his coffee, he exclaimed, "What??"

"Are you ever going to kiss me?" I repeated, "I'm just saying, we've gone out a few times, I've leaned in a few times, and I'm just wondering if you're ever going to kiss me?"

"Well, I can," he said.

"Well do you want to?"

"I just...well...um...you may have noticed that I'm a bit shy and awkward."

"Yes, I've noticed." I said.

"I just...well...um...it takes me a really long time to feel comfortable with someone."

"So, you're not going to kiss me?" I said.

And that was the end of that.

So I keep looking. I now have a new crush. He's thirteen years older than I am, already a grandfather, balding, with a bit of extra weight around his midsection. And yet when he looks at me, I forget to breathe. Is it possible? Could Yuri be my heavenly proclaimed?

Anonymous

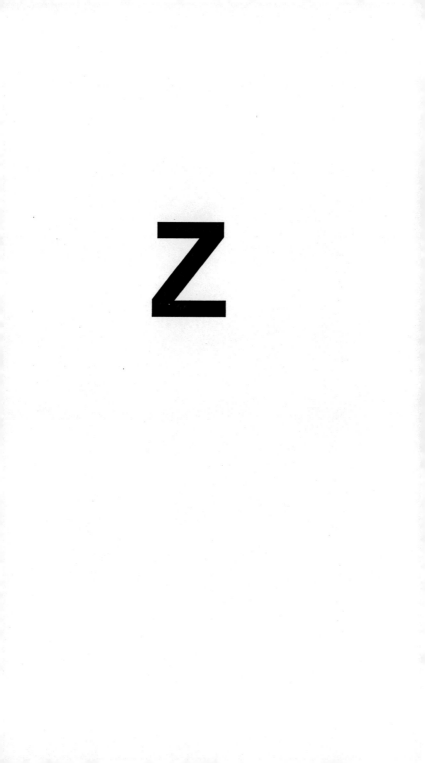

Z

Zach....

Zach(s) took over my summer. Over the course of last summer I had some sort of romantic encounter with eight (yes eight) Zachs. I ended a relationship with Zach in May and by August was set up on a blind date with another Zach. In the meantime I went on dates with three other Zachs, and said no to dates with yet another three Zachs. If you are confused, it's okay. We were too. I started numbering them – Z1-Z8!

Jennifer, 18

Zahir....

My girlfriends and I were standing in a long line at a club when all of a sudden this guy walked right up to the front of the line, got the bouncers attention and was about to get in. The bouncer came up to him and asked how many people were in the group. He said five, and I tapped him on the shoulder and said, "Don't you mean eight?" He looked at me, laughed, turned to the bouncer and said, "Actually, my party is eight."

Once we got into the club I didn't see him for the rest of the night so I assumed that he had left. I felt bad because I had wanted to buy him a drink for getting me and my friends in. At the very end of the night we saw him at the bar – I was about to go chat with him when I noticed that he was surrounded by other women. Not wanting to cramp his style I started to walk away when he noticed me and called me over. He ended up buying me a drink and we started talking. As it turned out we were both reasonably new to Toronto having both moved from the same city the year before! So, the random guy who got the random girl in the line into the bar turned out to be not so random after all. Months later we are still friends.

Candace, 33

Zane....

At what point can you assume that you're finally over someone or something? Or do some of the people or things that enter our lives settle so deeply within our beings that they will never be forgotten, no matter how hard we may try? Because I don't know if I will ever get over the someone, or something, that single-handedly changed my life forever.

I don't think about it as much anymore, so I suppose that should count for something. Maybe not.

It was late November. We were the only two people left at work after an early Christmas party for one of our clients. I flirted shamelessly as we scraped the left-over food into the garbage bins and collected the empty glasses and bottles. He flirted back. I still get butterflies just thinking about it. Harmless, I thought. Dangerous, I later found out. Our eyes met. I looked away. But my heart was pounding like a bass drum – what was I doing? He asked me what I'd like from the bar...on him tonight. I chose my favorite beer and he commented approvingly on my selection. We sat and talked with ease, finding each others' common interests. He asked about my life, I asked about his. It was the last time we'd ever talk like that, so innocent, so candid.

The room felt warm and close. The Christmas tree lights twinkled around us. It felt magical. That's what I remember most about it – the atmosphere, so perfectly romantic, a catalyst to our mounting body chemistry together. Perhaps if it were different, cold, uninviting, I could have avoided the trouble I was about to get myself into.

He got up, refreshed his beer. "Stairway to Heaven" came on the satellite radio station we were listening to. I felt like a teenager again – the nervousness, the adrenaline. I hadn't felt that sensation in so long.

When he kissed me it was as if the world suddenly collapsed, then disappeared. I don't remember exactly how it happened, just that one minute he was across the dimly lit room and the next he was standing over me, his face next to mine, his eyes, his cheek, his lips, his tongue...and there it was – the moral line, clear as day in front of me and just beckoning to be crossed.

I didn't walk. I ran across it. I kissed him back, hard and willing and wanting more so badly I couldn't breathe. And I didn't look back. Why was it so easy? Perhaps things that you think about, fantasize about often enough, even though you never truly expect them to happen, when they suddenly do, have such a fabricated place already lodged in your moral reality that you don't realize you're crossing the line at all. Of course that's just an excuse.

No excuse could possibly make up for how much I enjoyed what was happening to me right then and there – the lights, the warmth, the music, this beautiful man, loving me, wanting me, desiring me as much as I was desiring him. It was a catharsis. I wanted to scream. Strange though, that when you are in the act of doing something horrible, there exists no wrong in the world. I felt enlightened, exhilarated...

Hindsight is a brutal nightmare.

We continued our affair for six months before I couldn't handle the deception anymore and confessed everything to my husband. In the span of one hour I went from the most thrilling experience of my life, to the most awful hatred for myself and what I had done. I realized, now that it was over, the games that I had been playing and the extent to which I, myself, had been played. I considered myself one of the lucky ones because my husband stayed. But nothing ever heals those wounds. They sever and open when you least expect them. Not to mention the growing mistrust of your partner despite the fact that you're the one who committed the first offense. It never goes away.

As for the man who changed my life. He's out there somewhere, probably playing some other girl. Someday he'll realize his wrongs. But with me he was unapologetic. It doesn't stop me from hoping that one day he will try to contact me to tell me that he is sorry.

I didn't do what I did for revenge. I didn't do what I did to hurt anyone. I didn't do what I did because I was in love or out of love. But in the end, I know I did it for all of those reasons, and I ended up hurting myself. I was in love with the idea, and out of love with the person I was. I was trying to shake up my unhappy self-image. But the revenge I got on myself wasn't worth the pain of the process.

I don't know if I'll ever be over it. It's lodged too deeply in my heart. My mind. My being. The someone, the something, which changed my life forever. Me.

Jenna, 25

Check out the promotions and coupons from the partners of

rethink
breast cancer

Rethink Breast Cancer Canada
is a charity helping young people affected by and
concerned about breast cancer through innovative
education, research and support programs. Rethink
is a national volunteer-driven registered charity with
a bold, enterprising and entrepreneurial approach.

WE ARE THINKING DIFFERENTLY ABOUT
HOW TO BEAT BREAST CANCER.

BECOME A MONTHLY DONOR

**You can make a difference in the fight for the cause.
With your monthly commitment to Rethink Breast Cancer
you will support the future of our research and
awareness programs.**

Thank you for your support.

For more information and to find out how you can help please visit:
www.rethinkbreastcancer.com
296 Richmond St. West, Suite 301
Toronto, ON M5V 1X2
Tel. 416.920.0980 / 1.866.RETHINK

Proceeds from books sold during the
Stories From Our Black Books *release party and book-signing tour*
*will go to **Rethink Breast Cancer**.*

s·w·e·e·t·s·p·o·t·ca

It's easy to find...

You just need to know where to look.

Sweetspot.ca keeps you in-the-know about the sweetest offerings across Canada. From stores to sample sales, restaurants of the moment to hot events, the best bronzer to the perfect denim, sweetspot.ca is your source for all things, well, sweet.

Sign up now to receive your free daily Sweet Nothing email and you'll be up-to-the minute about everything that's fun, fashionable and just plain fabulous around town.

sister

underwear for fabulous girls

made in canada

Let your mouse do the shopping at
Toronto's only online collective
sheshoppe.ca!

Mail this coupon to:
She Shoppe
155 Coleridge Ave.
Toronto, Ont.
M4C 4H8
...and get your free She Shoppe lip gloss.

sheshoppe.ca

hip   .   funky   .   fun

ali
ENTERTAiNMENT

DANCE CAN MAKE YOUR CORPORATE PARTY, FAMILY EVENT, WEDDING, BAR MITZVAH OR ANY SPECIAL EVENT HAPPEN!

BOOK ONE OF THESE THREE THEMED DANCE PRODUCTIONS TODAY:

MAKE IT HAPPEN – A funky Hip Hop production that is ideal for any type of young or young at heart audience. Perfect for high energy, motivational or large scale events.

BELIEVE – A compilation of songs and movement that will encourage your audience to believe in themselves and what they are doing. Perfect for speakers series, weddings or any type of event where you are encouraging people to believe in themselves or a greater picture.

LIVE – An interactive presentation where two Hip Hop numbers are performed and then your entire audience will learn one of the two routines with our team. For the crowd who likes to live in the moment and experience through doing.

CALL ALI AND MENTION THIS COUPON AND RECEIVE 10% OFF LIVE, BELIEVE OR MAKE IT HAPPEN OR 10% OFF A PRODUCTION CHOREOGRAPHED JUST FOR YOU BY FAYE RAUW AND PERFORMED BY THE ALI TEAM.

Faye Rauw, originally from Saskatchewan, has been working professionally in the industry performing and choreographing for almost 15 years. Her TV and film credits include "Chicago" the movie, "Monk", "Sentinel", "Ham & Cheese" and the Bravo reality series "Strip Search". She's choreographed for recording artist Kristine W, Canadian launch of Britney Spears

FAYE RAUW
CREATIVE DIRECTOR
ALI ENTERTAINMENT

fragrance "CURIOUS", Canadian feature film "Forbidden Fruit". Steve Nash Charity Classic and various charities as well she has performed for U2, Royal Caribbean Cruiselines, Bell Mobility, Alitalia, Xerox, Coca Cola, Roots and many more. Currently, Faye resides in Toronto teaching dance & choreographing and is a proud Ambassador for Lululemon.

DANCE
makes IT
happen

416•850•0183
WWW.ALIENTERTAINMENT.CA

SERVE THIS!

A slice of a server's mind.

by Rima Maamari

Do you know what it's like to wait on tables?

Ever wonder what your server is thinking?

Order your copy today!

www.servethis.ca

Here are some of the critics
that are raving about this rant...

"The New York Times" "Breakfast Television/City TV" "Newstalk
1010 CFRB" "104.5 Chum FM/ Roger, Rick and Marilyn"

weconnect

women-owned businesses from a range of industries to exchange ideas and opportunities.

the interests of women entrepreneurs with the business community and government — at home and abroad.

women entrepreneurs to resources that will take their business to the next level.

WOMEN ENTREPRENEURS OF CANADA

get connected with Canada's leading not-for-profit organization dedicated to facilitating and championing women entrepreneurship. visit **wec.ca** today!

Printed in the United States
39111LVS00001B/1-108